ChangelingPress.com

Atlas/Warlock Duet
A Bones MC Romance
Marteeka Karland

Atlas/Warlock Duet
A Bones MC Romance
Marteeka Karland

All rights reserved.
Copyright ©2023 Marteeka Karland

ISBN: 978-1-60521-882-3

Publisher:
Changeling Press LLC
315 N. Centre St.
Martinsburg, WV 25404
ChangelingPress.com

Printed in the U.S.A.

Editor: Katriena Knights
Cover Artist: Marteeka Karland

The individual stories in this anthology have been previously released in E-Book format.

No part of this publication may be reproduced or shared by any electronic or mechanical means, including but not limited to reprinting, photocopying, or digital reproduction, without prior written permission from Changeling Press LLC.

This book contains sexually explicit scenes and adult language which some may find offensive and which is not appropriate for a young audience. Changeling Press books are for sale to adults, only, as defined by the laws of the country in which you made your purchase.

Table of Contents

Atlas (Iron Tzars MC 4) 4
    Chapter One 5
    Chapter Two 18
    Chapter Three 34
    Chapter Four 60
    Chapter Five 74
    Chapter Six 91
    Chapter Seven 107

Warlock (Black Reign MC 9) 115
    Prologue 116
    Chapter One 118
    Chapter Two 135
    Chapter Three 147
    Chapter Four 165
    Chapter Five 184
    Chapter Six 198
    Chapter Seven 212
    Chapter Eight 221

Marteeka Karland 236
Changeling Press E-Books 237

Atlas (Iron Tzars MC 4)
A Bones MC Romance
Marteeka Karland

Bellarose -- My drive to my new job didn't go as planned. Me and my "photographic memory" got lost, ending up on a private road in the middle of Nowhere, Indiana. Worse, I got a flat. And it was getting dark. When a dangerous, sexy biker stops to help, I'm not sure if I'm fortunate or not. Double that when I find myself mashed against said dangerous, sexy biker with him kissing me like he wants to devour me. Then things get really weird.

Atlas -- I'm in so much trouble. Not only is the girl in my care the most enchanting woman I've ever encountered, she's the daughter of one of the richest men in the world who happens to also be one third of the Shadow Demons. Which means, that kiss I stole might have signed my death warrant. Every instinct I have is telling me I need to call in my brothers to get her out and end the operation I've been deeply embedded in for months. But my little hellion has other ideas. I just hope we haven't waited too long. If I have, we're both dead.

Chapter One
Atlas

What a fucking mess. This fucking club in Terre Haute was rotten to the fucking core. I knew enough about it to make it implode with all the secret deals going on inside, but I hadn't been given the go-ahead from Sting, our president. Iron Tzars was an old MC, dating back to World War II. Back then, they'd been off-the-radar Nazi hunters. Meaning, they killed any they found and didn't ask permission from anyone to do it. Now we hunt down pedophiles and human trafficking rings. Occasionally we infiltrate domestic terrorist organizations, but most of those are on the government radar, and we let the FBI and ATF do their thing. This bunch, however...

They were as sadistic a bunch as I'd ever seen. Not only did they have their hands into the obligatory guns and drugs, the women and girls they took weren't trafficked. Oh no. They kept them. Used them. It had put me in a tenuous position because I couldn't keep my cover at the expense of innocents. With the help of my brothers at Iron Tzars, I'd managed to pull all of the under-aged girls out -- there weren't many, thank God. There were two other women still in the compound. One was happy to be there. Said so herself as she took one man after another with a smile on her face. The other one... wasn't in good enough shape to express her wishes.

That had been two months ago. Nothing had changed except I'd gotten the leader of this bunch to leave the unwilling woman alone. It wouldn't last long, though. The willing woman was fast becoming an unwilling woman. Which meant I'd run out of time.

I drove down the road back to the compound.

The bike I was on was an older chopper, but it was still a Harley, if heavily customized. It wasn't my own bike, but I tried to still treat it with respect. The meeting I'd just had, the plans being put into action, had me on the extreme edge. Which was likely why I nearly missed the woman crouched on her knees beside a new-model Ford on the side of the road.

I swerved, and I thought I heard her scream. Pulling over to the side of the road, I looked back over my shoulder. She was flat on her ass, gasping for breath. When she glanced in my direction, she scrambled to her feet and snagged the tire iron next to the car, holding it like a baseball bat.

With a scowl, I turned the bike around and drove the hundred feet or so back to her car before stopping and shutting it off.

"Did I hit you?" Despite my worries, I never wanted to hurt an innocent. The mere fact I hadn't seen her until I was right on top of her showed how distracted I'd been. A mistake like that could get me killed in this fucking club.

"I -- I..."

"Come on, girl! Are you hurt?" I snarled the question like a demand. Which it was. She took a step backward and rounded the back of the vehicle, putting the car between me and her.

"Don't come any closer! I know how to use this!"

I couldn't help but snort. "That thing probably weighs more than you do. Now, tell me if I hit you with the bike, li'l bit."

She shook her head slightly. "No."

I glanced at the driver's-side rear tire. Sure enough, it was flat. "Do you need help?" Again, she shook her head but didn't relax one bit. I sighed, scrubbing a hand over my beard. I didn't need this.

Not now. "Look. We got off on the wrong foot. I shouldn't have snarled at you. I didn't think I'd hit you, but even if I'd clipped you, you could have been hurt. It scared me as much as I scared you. Now. Are you sure you're OK?" I tried to soften my tone when it wasn't my nature. Women usually looked at my size, tats, beard, and muscles and ran straight into my arms, begging for a hard fucking. I had no interest in any woman who didn't.

"I'm fine."

I barked out a laugh. "I hate it when women do that, girl. You're not fine. I scared you to death."

"It's all right. You said it scared you too." Her voice was soft and lyrical, wrapping around my insides like silken ties. What the fuck was wrong with me? I wasn't hard up for female companionship. In fact, until I'd been planted in this fucking club, I'd had a different woman practically every night. More than one sometimes. Now, a little bit of timid innocence was burrowing inside me within a few seconds? Fuck...

"Not the point." I raised my open hands in a non-threatening gesture. "At least let me change your tire. Can I come closer?"

Finally, she lowered the tire iron slowly. "I suppose so. If you're sure you don't mind." She was so small I had doubts she could hold the damned thing for much longer anyway.

"I don't mind at all. It's the least I can do for nearly running you over. Besides, I don't leave women alone to fend for themselves. No matter how much they don't trust me." I'd meant the last to be a small joke. To lighten the mood. Because the fear on her face in the fading light hit me viscerally. I didn't like her thinking I'd hurt her or meant her ill will. That was the last thing I wanted after what I'd been through the last few months.

"I appreciate the help."

I knelt by the car, positioning the jack properly before inserting the jack handle and cranking to raise the car. "What are you doing on this road? It's pretty out of the way. Not many folks live around here." Because the club I was currently embedded in kept everyone out of their territory through terror and destruction.

"I got turned around," she said as she squatted beside me, holding the lug wrench at the ready. "I realized I was in the wrong place when the road went from four lanes to two. I don't remember passing another road, but I might have missed it."

"Where you headed?"

"Indiana State University. I was supposed to teach a summer class this session, but I got lost on the way to Terre Haute, then got lost trying to find the university. I'm supposed to check in tomorrow morning." I could hear her voice waver. One quick glance, and I saw her squeezing and kneading the handle of the lug wrench in a nervous gesture. "I'm sorry to be a bother. You'd still be on your way if I hadn't messed up all the way around today."

"Don't you have a phone with a maps program?"

"Um, yeah, but my phone's not really good. It died, and I haven't gotten a new one yet." She seemed to realize what she'd admitted to and tried to backtrack. "I mean, I think it'll still call 911 and stuff, but --"

"Relax, girl. I ain't gonna hurt you." I gestured to the tire I was trying to get changed before it got too dark to see. "I'm helpin' you. See?"

"Yeah." She gave a nervous laugh. "I guess you are."

I smiled. The girl really was lovely. Bit too innocent-looking for my tastes, but I could appreciate her beauty. "Come on. Let's get this done, and you can be on your way." While I worked, I gave her directions. She repeated them, asking questions about the area while I worked.

"What's your name, girl?"

"Bellarose."

I raised an eyebrow. "Bellarose. Got a last name?"

She bit her lip and let her gaze flicker away. "Um, Dane."

She was lying about something, but I wasn't sure what. Lying about her name didn't make much sense. There's no way in hell I could know her. Lord knew, if I'd met this woman before, I'd have remembered. She was small and slight but had curves in all the right places. Besides that, she was so lovely it made my teeth hurt.

I stuck out my hand to her before tightening the last nut. "Drake Pierce."

"Pleased to meet you, Mr. Pierce."

"Fuck," I chuckled, trying to put her at ease. "You make me sound like an old man. I know you're a young college hottie, but I'm only forty-one."

The smile she graced me with was nothing short of magical. Fuck, this girl was gorgeous! "Drake, then. Thanks for helping me. And for the directions."

Standing, I snagged the jack and lug wrench, putting them in the trunk of her car. "You remember how to get where you're going?" Bellarose rattled off the directions without hesitation. "Damn. That's some memory you've got there."

She grinned. "I've got something of a photographic memory. Not only can I remember everything I see or read, but when someone speaks, I kind of... I don't know. *See* the words. In my head." She tapped her temple. "It's why I felt comfortable continuing on when my phone died. I knew where I was going. At least, I thought I did." She frowned, glancing off. "I guess I'm not used to driving in bigger cities. Things look... different. You know. Different than just looking at a map. Shoulda read the directions instead of just looking at the map, I guess."

"If you'd known you wouldn't have access to the maps, I'm sure you would have. Anyway, this is a private road. You turned just a few hundred feet before you should have. This road used to be the main road into Terre Haute, but when they made the new one, the landowners extended the old road but blocked it off to make it private."

"I didn't see a sign, and there wasn't anything blocking it, or I'd never have turned in. There was a gate, but it was open. I thought it odd at the time but shrugged it off."

I knew she was telling the truth because Soul Reapers had opened it for ease of transportation for the meeting I'd just attended. Which brought me up short. I'd left before the other members had. There was a big party afterward, and I only participated enough to keep any suspicion down. The things they did at those parties made me want to kill a motherfucker. They had women practically begging to get inside, and the men liked to brag they could literally do anything they wanted to the women. Which was how the woman they now kept at the clubhouse had come to be with them. It would surprise me if Dutch didn't bring home a few more women with him since the young girls had "escaped." I wasn't sure how many more women or children I could safely protect on my own. It was time to call in my brothers.

"Well, now that you know, you shouldn't have problems next time."

"I hope not. It would be embarrassing if I didn't remember after I bragged about my memory." She smiled at me. I moved slowly so I didn't frighten her, standing close to her. Her eyes widened when I towered over her again, but she held her ground. She was still nervous, but she was trying.

"Good. Let's get you on your way, shall we?"

Only the jack remained to stow. She moved her luggage around to replace the jack in the trunk. Then she shut the trunk before sticking out her hand to me. "Thank you so much, Mister, uh, I mean Drake. I'm not sure I could have done this if you hadn't stopped to help me."

"Every woman needs to be able to change a tire if she has to. If you're gonna be out on your own, you need to learn. And a few other things about cars."

"I'll sign up for a class."

I wasn't sure if she was scoffing at me or not. Her smile, though, made me feel things I shouldn't. This wasn't the time, and it certainly wasn't the place. Not to mention this girl was half my age if she was a day. "I'll try to find you one."

"I'd offer you my number, but I have no idea if I'll be able to keep the same number when I get a new phone."

"It's fine. I'll just ask on campus for the teacher with the photographic memory when I find a class for you." Sweet God, that planted some decidedly erotic images in my mind.

Her laugh was even more distracting than her smile. Her hand in mine felt good. It was soft and delicate. Like the woman. She had straight, golden-brown hair that fell down her back past her waist, and wide hazel eyes. Her skin was a golden tan, and her lips a deep pink and plump. I could imagine taking that beautiful mouth in a lingering kiss.

Or having them wrapped around my cock...

I was about to open her car door for her when I heard the rumble of bikes coming from the meeting place.

"Fuck!" I turned my head and, off in the distance rounding a corner, I spotted headlamps and knew it was too late. The club was headed home, and this woman was directly in their path. There was no way to prevent her from being taken without blowing my cover. While I honestly could give a good Goddamn if it meant keeping her safe, me against twelve big, armed men trying to protect someone wasn't going to do either of us any favors. The only option I had was to take her with me, but to do that and keep everyone else away from her, I'd have to tell them she was my ol' lady, and they'd likely insist on making it official. Which meant we'd both be branded. Literally.

I weighed my options for a couple of seconds before making my decision. There was no way of fighting my way out of this situation. Not and get Bellarose out safely. I'd take her with me and regroup later.

"What's wrong?" She stepped closer to me, her hand going to my chest. Automatically, my arms closed around her and, despite the gravity of the situation, something inside me settled. This was where this woman was supposed to be. In my arms. Under my protection. I looked down at her and saw the moment she saw the group of motorcycles headed toward us. Her lips parted in a gasp and her breathing quickened. "Oh no. That's bad. Isn't it?"

"Yeah, honey. It's bad. Gonna need you to do exactly as I say. Don't speak unless I tell you to. Don't look directly at anyone. Keep your head down and do not leave my side. For any reason."

"What's going to happen?"

"Wish I could say. We both may be fucked, but I swear I'll fight to get you out. I know I have no right to ask, but I'm going to need you to trust me."

"I don't know you." Tears sprang from her eyes, and she trembled in my arms.

Unable to resist, I brushed a tear from under her eye as gently as I could. "I know, honey. If I could get you out of this before they got here I would. If you leave now, they'll follow. You're in their territory, so they can't afford not to. This is the only way. It's not going to be comfortable, but I'll protect you with my life. I swear it." She nodded, and more tears spilled over to drip down her cheeks. "In the eyes of the club, you're gonna be my woman. It will give me a reason to keep the others off you. But you have to do exactly as I say, Bellarose. If they don't think we're an actual couple, they will fight me outright for you. Do you understand?" Again she nodded, but her shivering intensified. No doubt she was scared as fuck and with good reason.

The group got closer, and I tightened my arms around Bellarose and brought my mouth down on hers in a gentle, coaxing kiss. I didn't want to scare her, but it had to be done.

Sweet God, she tasted good! I couldn't afford this. Not now. I had to keep my wits about me, but her kisses were fucking intoxicating! Even as terrified as she was, when I started kissing her, she stiffened slightly, gasped in a breath, then let out a contented sigh and just... let me have her. Her lips parted to let me sweep my tongue inside to tangle with hers. Her skin dampened, and her breath came in little pants. I'd bet my last dollar the girl had never been kissed. At least, not like I was doing. It made me an even bigger bastard for not only forcing the situation on her, but enjoying the pleasure of kissing her when it wasn't for the right reasons.

The closer they got, the harder I kissed her, needing to escalate things so Dutch would believe it was real. If I didn't do this all the way, there was no way Dutch would believe I was claiming her. If he didn't believe me, he'd try to take her. Might anyway. There would likely be a huge fight. There was no way I could lose that fight. With all the men in this group, I knew I couldn't win.

I tried to console myself with the fact that, if this worked, at least I wouldn't have to kill Dutch before I was ready. If I killed the prick before questioning him, I'd kill any chance I had of getting the contacts who were supplying him with girls -- or the other way around. If I lost those contacts, all these months I'd been inside this shit-stinking club would be for nothing. I hadn't survived the slimiest of the slimebags to lose the whole reason I was there. At least, that was what I told myself. I absolutely did not get a thrill out of making this girl mine, even if it was only for a short time.

The bikes pulled up to us and stopped. Men whooped and hollered as I continued to kiss Bellarose. The second she realized we had an audience, she stiffened, the commotion pulling her out of the moment. Now she was tense and scared, not at all looking like a woman with her man. These guys probably wouldn't notice. In their eyes, women didn't get a choice. A man wanted a woman, he took her.

Regardless of hers or anyone else's wishes. Dutch, on the other hand, would miss nothing. If he thought for a second Bellarose didn't want to be with me, he'd pounce.

I threaded my fingers through her hair at the back of her head and turned my body so I shielded her face. Pulling back just enough to part our lips, I whispered to her.

"Don't freak out. Follow my lead. As far as they're concerned, you're my woman. It's the only way to get us out of here safely, so you have to go along."

"I'm scared." Her little whimper tugged at my heart, but I couldn't comfort her the way she needed. "How do I know this isn't some ploy to get me to go quietly? You're kidnapping me, and you expect me to let you?"

"I know, honey. It looks bad. It *is* bad. Don't think about it right now. If you fight me, we're both dead, because I'll do my best to kill every motherfucker here to keep them away from you, and I'm vastly outnumbered. They'll kill me and make you wish they'd kill you." I brushed a gentle kiss over her lips once more, trying to soothe her when there was really no way to make her feel better about this. "We'll regroup the second we're alone. I'll call in reinforcements to help get you out of here. I won't let anyone hurt you, but you *have* to obey me. Instantly. No hesitation. Get me? And whatever you do, do not say a fucking word. Not even if I tell you to. We haven't gotten our stories straight yet, so you need to keep your mouth shut."

"O-Okay." She trembled in my arms. I kissed her once more before I finally turned my head to scowl at the other men.

"Don't you motherfuckers have any *fuckin'* thing

better to do?" I poured as much menace as I could into my voice. I'd played the crazy hardass for months now. Fucked up more than one of them when they'd disrespected me. Most of them backed off when I used that tone of voice now, but the president -- Dutch -- couldn't afford to show that kind of weakness. His assertiveness would give the others courage, and I couldn't have that. Bellarose flinched, but burrowed closer to me, her body trembling heavily.

"Could ask you the same thing, Atlas." Dutch scowled at me even as he eyed Bellarose. "Wha'cha got there? You know the rules. Share and share alike."

Immediately, the boys got in their two cents' worth.

"Yeah, I'd love to get my dick wet in that!"

"Looks like a hot little bitch. I want my turn."

"Fresh meat always tastes good."

Bellarose sounded like she tried to bite back a whimper, and her fingers bunched in my shirt, but she didn't make a sound or move otherwise. I knew she had to be terrified. Hell, even I wasn't at all comfortable with this, but I didn't have a choice yet.

The others always backed up the president. It wasn't so much a show of solidarity as it was to get their hands on the woman in my arms. Dutch grinned widely, thinking he had me.

"I don't share, Dutch." I ignored the byplay. The men had to be warned, but now wasn't the time. Once we got back to the clubhouse, I'd have to beat a few motherfuckers, but not here or now. "Pretty sure we've got shit to do at home. At least, if you want the shipment you just ordered." I kept it vague, knowing I'd get my point across while keeping Bellarose in the dark. Dutch would push the issue later, expecting an explanation for why she was on her way down a road where a secret meeting was being held. I'd have to figure that one out fast, because I had precious little time. If Dutch wasn't satisfied with my answer, we'd both be fucked. I also needed time for me and Bellarose to get our stories straight. Which I didn't have.

"Home we go, then," he said, a sadistic smile on his face as he continued to eye Bellarose. I was getting ready to have a fight on my hands to keep the girl.

Dutch wasn't the kind of man to take no for an answer with regard to anything in the club he wanted. Even the ol' ladies weren't out of bounds. I'd have to have some leverage to keep Bellarose, but I only had to buy us a few hours. Once I got back to my cabin, I could send out a signal to Wylde. He'd send back up, and I could maybe get Bellarose out right under the noses of the Soul Reapers. If it looked like Dutch was going to give me problems, I'd give the signal for my club to attack and we'd take what we had. But if I could force him into leaving Bellarose alone, I could finish this and save the lives of the women and children Dutch had just negotiated for at that meeting, *and* everyone else in the compound who didn't want to be there.

While it was wrong to force Bellarose to stay with me, to keep her prisoner, it was even more wrong to give up on those people when I was so close to rescuing them. At least, that's what I told myself. I had to keep a close eye on the risks versus the benefits on this one. I absolutely would not let Bellarose be collateral damage. And I wouldn't discount the fact that she was the first woman I'd ever met I could honestly say I needed for my own.

Chapter Two
Bellarose

I'd never been so scared in my life. Right up to the point where this man -- Drake? Atlas? -- kissed me. He didn't start out aggressively, but rather it felt like he was coaxing me to participate. And Lord knew I really wanted to participate. If I hadn't been so frightened, I would have enjoyed his kisses even more. Despite knowing there was immediate danger, Atlas didn't overwhelm me. Until the bikes approaching us stopped and revved their engines before shutting them down. Then he kissed me hard, thrusting his tongue deep once before turning his body to shield me.

When he did, he let up a little bit, his kisses turning coaxing once more. Damn the man, but he was potent! Even knowing the danger, it was hard to concentrate. I wasn't a virgin, but my sexual experience was limited for my age. I was twenty-five and had been with exactly one man. Never had I been kissed like this.

It was hard to process the conversation going on around me. All I could understand was that I was in deep shit. While Atlas wasn't the white knight I'd believed while he helped me change my tire, he hadn't hurt me. If this had been his goal all along, wouldn't he have handled things differently at the beginning? He could have taken me then. It sounded like he truly meant it when he told me he'd protect me from the others, so I had to believe his only intention at the time had been to help out a woman in trouble on the side of the road.

The men started up their bikes once again. Atlas took my arm and dragged me to his bike. He straddled it before taking my arm again to help me on. "Careful of the pipes. They'll burn you. Put your feet on the pegs."

"I've never done this." I kept my voice barely above a whisper. "My car --"

"Is just a car. We've got bigger problems to deal with. Right now, I need you to hang on to me as tight as you can. I'll take care of everything."

Atlas started up the bike before reaching behind him to run his fingers through my hair and pulling me forward for another kiss. Then he spoke against my lips once more. It was hard to hear him over the engine, but I caught it. "If they separate us, I'll do everything in my power to keep you safe. Including killing anyone who touches you. If they try to question you, keep your mouth shut. Don't say a single word for any reason. Not even your name. Not. One. Word."

I nodded, then he let go and revved his bike a couple of times before taking off. The one they called Dutch seemed to be in charge, and he pulled up beside us once we started down the road. Several times he looked at me and Atlas, a little smirk on his face. He gave me the creeps instantly.

I must have made a sound of distress because Atlas rubbed the outside of my thigh briefly as we flew down the road. Dutch still eyed us from time to time as we continued on but frowned at the familiar gesture.

When I shivered -- as much from fear as from the cool air as we cut through the night -- Atlas slowed down. Some of the bikes went on ahead of us, but Dutch stayed beside us, frowning at Atlas. Atlas turned his head briefly in Dutch's direction but didn't do anything else, only continued at the slower pace.

We pulled through a chain-link fence with a sliding gate, all of it topped with razor wire. I felt like I was being led into the gates of hell with no way out. I had to wonder if the man I clung to now was my savior or my captor. Perhaps he was both? I couldn't think about it yet. If I did, I was certain I'd dissolve into tears. Above everything else, I knew that showing that kind of weakness in front of these men would be a death sentence of the very unpleasant variety. All I could do was what Atlas told me. I'd have to trust in him to keep me safe. If he let me down? Well. At this point, I was dead anyway.

I suppose I could have gotten in my car and fled the second I realized we were in trouble, but though it was reliable and reasonably fast, there was no way my little Ford could outrun a motorcycle. I didn't have what it took to run someone down with my car even if they tried to force me off the road. They'd have had me anyway. At least I had Atlas standing in front of me. I did at the moment anyway.

Atlas started to go past the group of bikes that had stopped in front of us, but Dutch lazily rolled his bike between us and the rest of the group. I felt Atlas growl where I was mashed tightly against him. He shut down the bike but made no move to get off or to indicate I should move.

"Where you think you're goin'? Need to have us a discussion 'bout your little cherry there."

"Ain't got time for this," Atlas muttered. "So? Discuss!"

Dutch chuckled and shook his head. "Afraid not, man. We go inside where we can take our time." The double meaning wasn't lost on me.

"Already told you. I don't share."

"You can't take us all, Atlas. No matter how fuckin' big you are."

"Nope. But you're first on my list. After that, you won't care much what happens. I'm bettin' I can take more than two or three of the resta you with me too. So pick who dies first and come get me, motherfuckers." He pulled a gun from a shoulder holster and cocked it as he aimed at Dutch.

The other man chuckled as he held his hands up, like it was all one big joke. It didn't feel like Atlas was kidding, but I didn't know him. I held on to the belief that there was no need for deception from Atlas at this point. He had me where he wanted me, so I had no choice but to believe in him. Otherwise, what was the point of worrying? I was dead already.

"Just think we need to talk before we leave you to your own devices. I mean, even you'll admit havin' her show up on a closed road when we were meeting and discussing sensitive material is suspicious." The man's features hardened. "Makes me wonder if the two a' you's in cahoots. Tryin' to fuck with us."

The night got quiet. Every man in the area held their ground like they didn't dare to move. I saw several of them glance at each other, but no one moved or spoke.

"I suppose if you believe I ain't on the up and up, you should take your shot now." Atlas didn't move his weapon. "Still don't change the fact I'm gettin' you first."

Again, Dutch chuckled. "Come inside. We'll stash the bitch, and you and I can chat. You knew it would happen."

Atlas gripped my knee gently, a warning to stay silent. Which I knew meant he was going to give in to Dutch. I whimpered but quickly buried my face in his wide back. He rubbed my knee slowly up and down in a soothing manner. This was going to be a serious test of my trust. Or my intelligence. Because I wasn't altogether certain I'd done the intelligent thing so far.

Without looking back at me, Atlas held out his hand. I took it as my cue to get off the bike. One hand on his shoulder, one in his hand, I swung my leg over, careful of the pipes. Atlas didn't let go of my hand as he dismounted. He also kept his gun in his right hand, even though he'd lowered it.

He followed Dutch inside, keeping a firm grip on my hand. There were several men inside along with three women who were either completely or mostly naked. The men called out a greeting to the group entering the room. Dutch ignored everyone, moving through the room at a brisk clip. Atlas kept up with him easily, but their long strides caused me to have to jog to keep up. Catcalls broke out around the room.

"We all gettin' a piece of that. Right?"

"Nice little innocent. You're 'bout to have your world rocked, little girl."

Catcalls followed me as I was practically dragged across the room, but I had my instructions. Not one word. And, really. That was sound advice as well as an order. The only thing speaking would do for me was piss off the wrong people or make them even more determined to have some fun with me. For the first time since I'd left home in Rockwell, Illinois, I understood why my mother and adopted father hadn't wanted me on my own. Alexei was used to this world. He lived in it when he interacted with the various MC's he supplied with smart weapons. Giovanni made the weapons using the tech created by Argent Tech, an international juggernaut. They didn't make the weapons, but the tech that went into them. Anything the Shadow Demons supplied to the motorcycle clubs/paramilitary organizations in their circle was created by Giovanni. I was also deeply regretting getting rid of the expensive phone Dad had given me in favor of a cheap version that was functional but free of Giovanni's meddling.

"The boys'll look after your new toy, Atlas." Dutch grinned as he unlocked the door to what looked like an office.

"You know that's not happenin'. She stays with me."

"No can do. And if you've already made her privy to our secrets..."

"I don't work that way, Dutch. She doesn't know anything about our business, and I'll keep it that way. But I'm not leaving my woman in the tender care of the club men."

Dutch raised his eyebrows. "Your woman? You didn't mention anything about having a woman."

"Not your business."

"It is when she compromises a secret meet." Dutch looked from Atlas back to me. I did my best to follow Atlas's command and keep my eyes down, but it was hard. If the other man came for me, I wanted to have time to react. The last thing I wanted was for him to get his hands on me. I had a feeling I wouldn't survive it.

"She didn't know there was a meet... until you told her. Nice job, prez."

Dutch lunged for Atlas, swinging a punch. Atlas didn't even flinch, catching the man's meaty fist in his hand with an audible slap. I flinched, but kept my gaze on the floor, hoping not to catch Dutch's attention after his show of temper.

Dutch's explosion wasn't what startled me, though. It was Atlas's casual use of strength. I'd have bet money Dutch put everything he had into that punch, and Atlas caught it like the other man was a scrawny teenager having a tantrum.

"You get that one for free, Dutch. Take another swing at me, and I'll retaliate." Atlas still had my hand firmly in his, his body a shield between me and Dutch. I tried to let go, putting my other hand in the waistband of his jeans in case he had to fight the other man, but Atlas held tight. "You want to talk? We'll talk. But I'm not putting my woman in danger to do it."

Dutch jerked his head to the right, indicating a closed door. "Put her in there. You can lock it and keep the fuckin' key."

Atlas led me to the door in question. He removed the padlock hanging from the ring of the hasp lock that secured it closed. My heart pounded as he opened the door and shoved me gently inside.

He gave me a hard look. "Remember what I said. Not a sound." His murmured command brooked no argument. There was no light, and as he shut the door, I couldn't help the little whimper that escaped. It was near total darkness, and the only light came from under the door. I heard him sliding the lock into place and clicking it together.

The brief glimpse I'd had of my surroundings told me I was in some kind of a supply closet. I backed up until I felt the wall at my back. I felt out with my right hand to where I thought a broom or mop was propped. When my palm circled the cool wooden handle, I brought it close and gripped the handle in front of me in both hands. Then I slid down the wall, making myself as small as possible. I thought I was next to some large buckets but wasn't sure if that was what they were. Either way, I scooted behind them for protection. If nothing else, maybe the brief seconds it took someone to locate me when they opened the door would give me enough time to either attack or run. Or both.

Never in my wildest nightmares had I imagined a scenario like this. If they'd known who my father was, maybe. They'd want to hold me for ransom or something. But out of the blue? Just because I was in the wrong place at the wrong time? No. Fucking figured, though. My car was likely long gone, my purse and any money I had gone with it. I needed to figure out a way to get Giovanni's attention, but without a debit card or using any of the accounts I had access to, he had no way of finding me. Preferably before Dutch or anyone else in the club found my driver's license and put two and two together. My only hope was that Atlas lived up to his promise to keep me safe. The way my luck was going, I couldn't rely on him. Not for long, anyway.

In a word? I was fucked.

* * *

Atlas

It nearly gutted me to lock that girl in the closet, but I did it. I heard her whimper, but she held it together. At least for now. I turned and faced the group of men outside Dutch's office. "Anyone even thinks about breakin' that lock and makin' a try for her, his death won't be quick. Or clean."

More than one of them raised his hands and backed off, but a couple of Dutch's inner circle sneered at me. I stared them down until, one by one, they turned to leave.

"My, someone has it bad." Dutch was observant, but even he didn't realize the extent of what I'd do to protect Bellarose. I kept telling myself she was innocent in all these games, but it wasn't that. At least, it wasn't *only* that.

"She's mine. End of discussion. Talk about something else." I was losing my patience with the bastard.

"Fine." He waved his arm to indicate I should go into his office. I waited, giving him a steely glare until he finally barked out a laugh and entered ahead of me. No way I was putting that fucking psycho at my back. I'd put myself in a position where he needed me more than I needed him, but Dutch didn't really give a shit. If I proved too much for him to handle, he'd off me without a moment's hesitation. Or try to. It was why I always kept my eye on him.

"So," he said, seating himself at his desk and propping his feet up. "Tell me what brings your bitch into my territory."

I shrugged. "I asked her to come to me. I intended to meet her at the end of the road, but she got here early. She didn't realize she was in your territory, because I didn't tell her. Since she had to wait, she tried to get off the main road so no one saw her and came to investigate."

"I'm sure she'll corroborate your claims."

"Of course. But you're not questioning her alone. No one goes near her without me being there."

"I'm hurt you don't trust me, Atlas." I wanted to wipe that fucking smile off Dutch's face. He was a bastard sent straight from hell, and I wanted with everything in me to send him back there.

"I don't trust anybody with what's mine."

"Fine. Take your little pet and go to your cabin. I'll be watching you, Atlas. This is a serious breach of security, and I won't have this deal compromised."

"I've been here for months, Dutch. Have I compromised security yet? In fact, didn't I find more than one trusted member of your club who'd been willing women here without this horseshit." That wouldn't stop them for long, but it might work for a while. Didn't make me any friends, but I could live with that.

"But the women know why they're here. They agree to it when they get in!" someone whined, but I was done with this. "Then tell Bozz, and he'll kick her out of the compound. She changes her mind and says no, she doesn't get to stay, but you still don't get to fuck her. Simple."

There was grumbling around the room, but I could tell they were going to do as I said. At least for now. If only it were as easy with Dutch's private "collection." There was at least one woman in real trouble and another one about to revoke her consent. They were two of the women I needed to get out of this hell hole. So much was riding on my shoulders. I didn't need anything else. Running into Rose when I did was both a blessing and a curse. I could keep her safe, but how much would it cost? Yet, if I hadn't taken her as my woman, she would have been at the mercy of this bunch. And what I'd done for the woman who'd crumpled beside the pool table would have been all I could have done for Rose. That thought, more than anything, turned my stomach like nothing had since I was a boy.

Bellarose didn't say anything else. Instead, she followed me outside and climbed on my bike when I told her to, and we took off. My cabin wasn't far from the main house, but close enough to the woods and the outer perimeter that I could get out if I needed to. Theoretically.

I knew there were men watching me, but I'd managed to gain enough trust with Dutch, and I'd pointed out some of the men wanting leadership of the club. That had reduced the number of eyes on me considerably. Reminding him tonight of the dissension in the ranks had been all about reminding him I'd had his back. We weren't friends by any means, but he'd brought me in to do a job. Root out the dissension and help set up this pipeline of human trafficking. To Dutch, it looked like I'd done exactly that. What he didn't know was that the people who were in place to help move his cargo were plants either from my own club or the Shadow Demons.

I didn't say anything as I helped her from the bike and took her hand to lead her inside my cabin. Music was blaring from the inside. The place was fucking crappy, but I kept it as clean as I could and was thankful I had the cabin instead of a room inside the clubhouse. We'd have been lucky to last the night staying in the middle of the club. At least this way, I had better control. I could get a warning if anyone tried to break in.

Thanks to Sting, our president, we'd negotiated some micro cameras from Giovanni Romano with the Shadow Demons. I had them set up all around the house. I had the app he'd developed set to alarm me if anything got within fifty yards of the house. I occasionally got passersby, but for the most part, anyone close enough to be picked up by the app was too fucking close.

I shut the door and locked it. It only had one deadbolt, but honestly, the door was shit. Just like the cabin. If anyone wanted in, they were getting in. The only reason I locked it was to give myself precious extra seconds if it became necessary. Instead of turning around, I rested my forehead on the door, trying to get myself under control. If I turned around and saw her right this second, I wasn't sure I wouldn't try to kiss her again. If I kissed her in the place I'd called home for several months, I was definitely fucking her.

She was quiet, not even breathing hard. Was she scared? What was I thinking -- of course she was scared. Who wouldn't be in this situation?

I walked over to a radio I had sitting on a shelf over the counter next to the stove, turning it down slightly. I always had some obnoxious metal playing. The guitars screamed like chainsaws, and the drums were heavy. Any lyrics were screamed and exceedingly loud. It wasn't comfortable, but it kept out prying ears.

Rose scrunched her nose. I got it. Not only was the music loud, but it grated on every single nerve a person had. I basically tuned it out most days, but she wasn't used to it.

I put my finger to my lips, indicating for her to stay quiet. She nodded once, and I took her hand, leading her to the couch. I put my arm around her shoulders, and she looked up at me, a mixture of fear and longing etched in her lovely face. I felt sure she expected me to kiss her and wasn't sure how she felt about it. For the briefest of moments, she'd enjoyed my kiss. I knew I could make her enjoy more than kisses, but not like this.

"You're basically my prisoner, Rose. I'm not kissin' you again." I spoke softly. The whole point of the horrid "music" was to cover anything I said or did.

A brief flash of hurt passed over her face, and she looked away, a blush creeping up her neck to her cheeks. She shook her head. I wasn't sure what she meant, but I took it to mean that, yeah. No kissing.

I leaned in and put my lips at her ear. "Never talk freely anywhere inside the compound. You're always watched and listened to. Understand?" She shivered but gave a short nod. "We need to get our story straight. Dutch will question you at some point, though I'll be with you. You are not to say a word. Nothing. You nod when I tell you to. You *never* speak." Again, she nodded. "Good. I called you to meet me at the entrance to that road. You arrived early and didn't want anyone to see you parked there, so you drove down the road a short way to hide your car. That's it." Another nod. "Good. Next thing is, if I leave this cabin without you, you are to stay inside. You do not answer the door. You stay out of sight of the doors and windows when you can. If someone breaks in, you'll have a panic button of sorts. It will let me know there's trouble, and I can access cameras inside and outside the cabin and see what you're up against so I can be prepared before I enter." Nod. "Last thing, and I'm repeating myself because it's important. *Say. Nothing.* If you're not sure what to do, look to me, but no matter what, you say nothing."

She moved her lips to my ear. Her breath feathering over my sensitive skin made me shiver this time. Instantly, my cock was aching and pulsing like mad. I was so fucked. "How long?"

I shrugged. "Not sure. Hopefully not more than a couple of days. I'm callin' in my club early. But I have time to make a controlled exit so I can get the other women out."

"I'm sorry, Atlas. I'm not sure what I messed up, but I'm aware your job is now more difficult."

"It is, but I wouldn't have it any other way. The alternative is them chasin' you down. You'd be in their hands now instead of mine."

She nodded, then pointed to the bathroom.

"Leave any towels or rugs exactly where they are. I found holes in the walls and floors and covered

Again, there was a knock. "Rose. I need you to come out."

At the sound of Atlas's voice, I let out a relieved sob but quickly bit it back. I jumped up and went to the door, unlocking it and opening it slowly so I could peek out.

"Come with me," he said, holding out his hand. He gave me a steady look, and I didn't dare take my gaze from his. He nodded once -- approval? -- then led me to the threadbare couch where we sat. Atlas put an arm around my shoulders possessively and crossed one ankle over the opposite knee. "Rose, this is Bozz. He's the sergeant at arms for the Soul Reapers. He has questions for you."

I looked up at Atlas, my eyes wide. Hadn't he told me not to answer? Even if he told me to? I was to keep my mouth shut no matter what. My breath came in sharp pants as my anxiety rose, but I didn't make a sound. I bit my lip and turned into Atlas's body, shamelessly hiding my face in his shoulder.

Atlas wrapped his other arm around me, rubbing my upper arm up and down in a soothing gesture. "It's OK. I'm here, and I'm not leaving."

"Christ, Atlas." Bozz scowled and scrubbed his hand over his lower face and beard. "Knew you liked submissives, but this is a bit much even for you. Can she even talk?"

Atlas shrugged. "The only thing she needs to do with her mouth doesn't involve talking. Besides, the man I bought her from assured me she'd learned her lesson about speaking in public. Or to anyone other than me -- since she's mine -- and only when I require an answer from her."

"Well, require it now!" Bozz slammed his fist down onto the arm of the chair across from where

Atlas and I sat. "Dutch wants answers."

"I gave him an answer."

"I need to hear it from her."

"Even if I give her permission, she's not going to talk. She doesn't speak. Rarely even to me." When the other man growled his frustration, Atlas continued. "Look at it this way. If she doesn't talk to anyone, she can't repeat anything she sees or hears."

"How do you know she won't turn on you?"

"Because I'm her master." Atlas delivered that punch with an evil grin. I glanced up at him before clutching his shirt and turning against his shoulder once more. All I had to do was keep my mouth closed.

Bozz snorted. "Lots of men think they're masters over their women. In my experience women are more wily than you realize. She could snap. Stab you in your sleep. Any number of things. I'm gonna need more than that."

"She's completely loyal to me. Wouldn't have taken her as my woman if she wasn't."

"Never met a woman that loyal."

"Of course not. As I said. She'd been properly trained. She doesn't speak in front of others. She doesn't defy me. She'd die for me if I required it. I take care of her. Protect her. She behaves as she knows I require, even when pressured."

"This isn't what you discussed with Dutch. He said I could question her as long as you were with her."

Atlas shrugged. "I said that almost exactly. Didn't say she'd answer any questions. Just that no one got to be alone with her."

"You're on thin ice." Bozz stabbed a finger at Atlas. "Dutch ain't gonna like this."

"He doesn't have to. But he better fuckin' accept

it."

Bozz picked up something he'd sat on the floor. I realized it was my purse when he tossed it to the couch beside Atlas. "Got it out of her car. Ain't much in there. Now." Bozz flashed a grin at Atlas. It wasn't a pleasant look. "Expect to be watched from now until Dutch is satisfied you're not a threat to him."

"Oh, make no mistake, Bozz. I'm a fuckin' threat. You tell him that's your takeaway from this meeting. Now get the fuck outta my space."

With a disgruntled snort, Bozz did as he was told. I got the feeling that wouldn't be the end of it, though. Bozz didn't bother to shut the door as he left. Atlas rose and crossed the short distance to the door to shut and lock it, then pulled out his phone and watched the screen.

Several seconds later, he held up the phone, then pointed outside. He crossed to the radio and, once again, turned it up with that obnoxious music. I grimaced but understood the need. Any listening devices would be seriously hampered by the plethora of frequencies and sounds.

The cabin was small, and the only separate room off the main room was the tiny bathroom. It was surprisingly clean, though slightly messy. The small, unmade bed was shoved up against a wall out of the main area in a corner. It allowed for some privacy, but not much. Then again, with only one man living here he had all the privacy he needed, I guess.

He took my hand and led me away from the couch to the bed, where we sat. Then he leaned in to me, kissing my neck and collarbone. I couldn't help but shiver. I was scared, but the danger combined with the potent, charismatic man turned me on more than it should have. *Way* the fuck more than it should have.

He urged me onto the bed, then lay beside me on his side, away from the couch where we'd just sat and pulled me close. Once again, he put his lips by my ear, and I knew this was all for show.

"You did good. That's what you do from now on. Always stay close to me and don't say a word, no matter what." I nodded, and he rolled over to wedge his hips between my legs before taking my mouth in another scorching kiss.

I whimpered in both fear and arousal. The combination was a conundrum I couldn't reconcile in my head. I was terrified this man would take something from me I wasn't willing to give, but his kisses were so intoxicating I wasn't sure I'd really put up a fight if he did. Then he spoke to me, his lips still against mine. Again, his voice was so soft I could barely catch the words, but it was clear he thought we were being monitored.

"I'm sorry, little Rose." Everyone always called me Bella, but I liked that he'd shortened my name to Rose instead. "I know I said no more kissing, but I'm not going to hurt you, and I'll never take anything but a few kisses." He stroked my hair off my cheek as he took another kiss. "But Bozz planted a camera on the chair over there. It's small and not noticeable unless you're looking for it, but it's there. I'll show you in a bit. He and Dutch have to believe we're together, or we're both in trouble."

"I'm scared." I whispered the plea against his lips like he'd spoken to me.

"You'd be a fool if you weren't. You want me to lay this out for you so you know what we're up against?" Atlas was deliberately referring to us as a team.

"That's a tactic to get me involved in whatever

you're doing. Or at least what you want me to think you're doing."

"It is." It surprised me that he didn't try to deny it. "As much as I want you out of here and to safety, I can protect you if you do exactly as I say. There are other women here -- like the woman in the clubhouse -- and I can't help them all."

"Tell me, and I'll judge for myself."

Keeping my leg around his hip, he rolled us to our sides, so his back was to the chair he'd indicated. "This club is deep in negotiations to move women and children into a trafficking ring. I'm trying to stop them."

"How?"

"I have people in place ready to act as the buyers to get these women out, but the bigger plan will take longer. I'm embedded in this club for the long haul. My goal is for them to lead me to the buyers Dutch is really trying to hook up with. If I call in my team, they rescue this group of women *only*. Taking down the men Dutch claims to know will set free dozens of women and children in several different counties."

"Can't you get us out and continue on after that?"

"That would mean putting more women at risk of being abducted by Dutch and his men in the meantime. Right now, he's got all he can safely handle without risk of discovery. I think he's close to getting the meet he wants. Once he does, my team will know who to target and, once they confirm they have all the innocents to safety, they can come in and kill these motherfuckers."

"A permanent solution?"

He nodded slowly, his eyes narrowing. I knew what was coming. And, really, if Atlas was on the up and up, he needed to know who I was.

"That doesn't faze you. Does it." It wasn't a question.

"I'm afraid not. I'm not used to being around MCs all the time or, especially, ones as black as this one seems to be, but I know how they operate and that they usually make their own rules to suit their own moral code."

"Tell me what you're hinting at, girl."

I took a breath and leaned in closer. "If anyone finds out who I am, we're both dead. At least, we are if you meant what you said about protecting me with your life. Telling you who I am makes me incredibly vulnerable."

"Not askin' again, girl."

"My name is Bellarose Dane-Petrov." I let it linger there, waiting to see if he had a reaction at all. If there was any way to keep from voicing out loud that my father was one of the owners of the most powerful tech company in the world, I'd like to take it.

He was silent for a long moment, staring at me with his brows knitted together. Then he jerked back like I'd struck him before rolling over on top of me again. "Are you fuckin' kidding me?" His snarl made me cringe, and I had to bite back a whimper. I was on this man's good side so far, but if that ever changed, I was going to be in a hell of a spot. Atlas wasn't a man I ever wanted to cross. "If you're fuckin' lyin' to me, I'll beat your ass, girl."

"Alexei Petrov is my father."

"*Step*father." My gut was churning as he tried to clarify my actual relation to the infamous leader of the Shadow Demons. The look on his face seemed to ask, "Could this fucking night get any worse?"

"He adopted me and has never treated me as

anything less than his daughter. I don't remember my biological dad, so he's the only father I've ever known. How did you know my relationship to him?"

"My club has a dialogue with the Shadow Demons. Your name has been mentioned from time to time. Bellarose is a unique name, but they usually call you Bella. Don't they?"

"Yes."

"Fuck," he swore softly before rising and turning away. He went to the bathroom and shut the door, not saying another word to me. The music still blared, but I didn't dare get up to turn it down. I got the feeling Atlas was riding a fine line at the moment. I didn't blame him. This had to be his worst nightmare. When my dad found out about this, he was going to crush everyone in the vicinity and fuck the collateral damage. I knew my dad. He'd have no remorse if it meant I was safe.

* * *

Atlas

Fucking motherfucking Goddamned fucking shit! And piss!

I had no idea what to do. OK, that wasn't true. Scrubbing a hand over my face, I shoved away from the sink and went to a place over the water heater where I'd hidden a sat phone. Giovanni Romano, the tech guy all tech guys aspire to be, had assured me the satellites the phone used made it impossible for the call to be traced. Giovanni was a cocky son of a bitch, but he was a genius with anything technical, and I trusted he knew what he was talking about. And it was a good thing, too, because I was about to trust him with my fucking life. And the life of Alexei's daughter.

I made the call and waited patiently while it

connected. When it was answered, the voice on the other end of the line asked, "You good?"

"No. We have a problem."

The president of my club, Sting, answered, thank God. knew we needed to keep the conversation short. No sense taking more risks than absolutely necessary.

"What do you need?"

How to answer that? "We may have to take option two."

"How soon you need it?" No hesitation or questions. He'd do whatever I indicated needed to be done.

"Give me a couple of hours. I'll contact you again. If you don't hear from me by then, move."

There was a pause, then Sting acknowledged. "Copy."

I hung up the phone. Two hours. I had two hours to make a decision. That was assuming Dutch hadn't figured out who this girl was. He'd had her purse, and they'd obviously searched it. They'd have found her license. If the license had her name listed as Petrov, we were screwed. If it had her listed as Dane, we might have a chance. I'd need to find that out now.

I replaced the phone before storming out of the bathroom. Music still blasted from the speakers. Rose sat on the bed where I'd left her, looking pale and frightened. With good reason.

Scrubbing my hand over my face, I went to her, ever mindful of the camera Bozz had planted. Reaching out my hand to her and keeping my back to the camera, I spoke slowly so she could read my lips over the music if necessary. "Let's get something to eat."

She glanced nervously toward the chair and nodded, not saying a word. I raised my eyebrow as she took my hand and followed me meekly. Unless she was a complete dumbass, she was playing the part I'd set for her to perfection. Given the fact she was Alexei Petrov's daughter -- even if she was adopted and not his biological child -- I knew there was no way Rose was a dumbass.

The one thing that did surprise me, though, was how calm she seemed. I knew she was probably a wreck inside -- what woman wouldn't be in this situation? But she held it in and did exactly what I told her to. It was that fact alone that had me waiting those two hours to call in my brothers. There was a possibility I could set up safeguards in the event we were discovered so I could continue with this operation. If Rose could continue to play the part as well as she had with Bozz, we could do this. But did I have the right to ask her to?

We stepped outside the house, the music continuing to blare inside. Rose looked up at me and raised an eyebrow. Wanting to know what was happening but continuing to play her part.

"First question. Does your license have your name listed as Petrov?" When she shook her head, I let out a breath I hadn't realized I'd been holding. "Good. They might not put you together with Alexei. Since you're still here with me and they haven't tried to take us by force, odds are they haven't. This outing is a test. Then we have some decisions to make. We'll give it an hour, then head back. We're going to eat. I'm testing the waters, so you need to continue like you're doing. Which is perfect, by the way. Just keep it up." She closed her eyes briefly before nodding. "You stay with me. You do not leave my side for any reason. If I'm not holding your hand, you put yours in the waistband of my jeans. Got it?" She nodded without hesitation.

"Good. You got this." Again, she nodded. I tried to sound encouraging but wasn't sure I pulled it off.

I took us back to the clubhouse area. The guys grilled burgers and dogs in the evening while they drank and got high. There was always a lot of fucking going on with the women hanging out with the club. I didn't want Rose too near the action, but I had to be seen with her. It was all to make an appearance like I did every night. If I didn't show, there would be suspicion, though I could cover it with wanting time alone with my woman. It would still probably look out of character and I wasn't willing to chance it yet. Once they got used to seeing me with Rose, I'd reevaluate. It was also the perfect way to test Rose in an environment where it wouldn't be a complete disaster if she messed up. It might cause me to have to punish her in public, but I could fake that for the most part if I had to.

We arrived, and I got us a couple of plates, staring down any of the men who shot glances our way or hollered out catcalls to Rose. To her credit, she didn't rise to the bait. Instead, she kept her gaze down and her hand either in mine, or in the waistband of my jeans.

I found a spot on a picnic table next to the bonfire in the back of the yard. Instead of having Rose sit beside me, I positioned her between my legs on the ground. At first she got a disgruntled look on her face, but she kept her head down and didn't so much as flinch when I pressed on her shoulders until she was seated.

"You can rest your arms on my legs if you want. I'll feed you while you watch everything around you. Learn the men in the area. The women. Figure out who the most dangerous person in the place is. Do all that and still be demure. You don't make eye contact. Remember?" She nodded, glancing up at me with a determined look.

Fuck me. That look hit me like a baseball bat to the balls. I knew by the expression on her face and in her eyes, she would do exactly what I told her to. She'd also be accurate in her assessments. For the first time since I'd realized I'd have to take Rose with me back to this hell hole, I had hope that I could complete this task. I could wait out Dutch and the men he was trying to work out a deal with just like I'd planned.

The thought had just crossed my mind when I saw the man in question stalking toward me. Bozz wasn't far behind. I handed Rose a bite of hot dog and gave her a steady look as she bit the dog from my hand.

"Show's on, sweetheart. Make me proud."

And there went that look again. My cock ached like a motherfucker as Rose continued to stare up at me like an adoring pet. It made me the worst kind of bastard, but I held the hot dog to her lips again, encouraging her to take another bite. As Dutch and Bozz stopped beside us, she took one slow bite, never breaking eye contact until she started to chew. Then she lowered her gaze and laid her head on my thigh, facing the two men. Yeah. She was good.

"Well, I see the appeal of your little pet now." Dutch leered at Rose, licking his lips like he was dying for a taste. "Might have to sample her charms for myself."

"Not if you want to keep your dick attached to your body." I gave Dutch a level look. The man just chuckled.

"I must say, I never thought I'd see you in this position. Never thought you had it in you to care for a woman, Atlas."

"I never said I cared about her. I said she was mine. No one takes something that belongs to me."

"Watch your tone, motherfucker," Bozz snarled. "He's the president. Not you."

"I was doing him a courtesy by warning him. Most men I'd simply cut for coveting what's mine. I don't share. Ever."

"Much as I'd like to... negotiate with you on this, I have more important things to discuss. Once this is over, we'll revisit your willingness to let me have a taste of your little pet."

"What do you want, Dutch? I want to get back to my cabin and fuck."

He shrugged. "So? Fuck her. We won't mind." I just glared at the other man. "All right, all right." Dutch put his hands up in surrender with a light chuckle. "Don't get your panties in a wad." Then he sobered. "I heard back from my source today. I'm supposed to talk with Swede in two weeks. If all goes well, we can offload the cargo we have within a month. I need you to be ready to help with the transport, and the negotiation. Get me top dollar for them."

I shrugged. "You want top dollar, they can't be used and beaten. They'll need to be fed regularly and allowed to rest. You can't let the men fuck them at their whim like you been doin'."

Dutch narrowed his eyes. "You tellin' me how to run my club, Atlas?"

"Nope. I'm tellin' you how to get top dollar for your cargo. I could give a good Goddamn how you run your fuckin' club. Or how you treat your cargo, for that matter. You're payin' me to get the most bang for your buck, so I'm tellin' you how to do that. Makes no difference to me if you take my advice or not. I just want it known that I warned you."

Bozz had been studying me the whole time, and he nodded "Ain't sure how much of his horseshit I believe 'bout him not caring how we treat the women, but what he says makes sense."

"You got a soft spot for the ladies?" Dutch tilted his head, studying me.

"Makes no difference to me what you do. But no. I don't enjoy seeing men hurt women just to see 'em hurting. You want to beat up on someone? Pick on someone your own size. Only a pussy beats on someone smaller than him."

Bozz growled and took a step forward. I continued to feed Rose the hot dog. She seemed to ignore everything around her other than me, but judging by the glimpses I got of her face, I could tell she was taking it all in like I'd told her to.

"Easy, Bozz." Dutch moved between me and Bozz, keeping us separated.

"I'll do whatever I want to the bitches," Bozz snapped. "He don't get to tell me what I can do or who I can fuck in my own fuckin' club!"

"Back off, Bozz. Go find a club girl and fuck some of that aggression away. But lay off the merchandise. I want as much money out of those bitches as he can get me." Money was the only thing I could think of to get Dutch to make the guys lay off the women. Seemed it worked for the time being. I knew it wouldn't last, though.

Dutch had wisely only let a close circle of his men in on this scheme, but even that lot wasn't as disciplined as they should be. Not for something like this. They let their impulses rule them. Dutch did too, but his greed helped keep him in check. For now.

As Bozz stomped off, Dutch's gaze moved to

Rose. If the man figured out who she was, we'd be in big trouble. I was mindful of the time for a couple of reasons. I didn't want my team jumping in yet, but I also wanted to know exactly how much time I had if things went bad and I wasn't able to signal them to stand down.

"Your woman settling in?" Dutch's smile was greedy, leaving no doubt he wanted Rose. When I gave him a steady glare, he continued. "Because I'll be happy to help if she isn't."

"Ain't tellin' you again, Dutch. I don't share."

"All right, all right. But I want her when you're done." He leered at Rose. She shivered slightly but didn't look up or acknowledge the man in any other way.

"I'll be gone from this shit-hole long before then. I'm here to help with this deal. Then I'm gone."

Dutch shrugged. "Unless I need you further." The intent was clear. Dutch wanted his taste of Rose, no matter how long it took. Which was trouble. The longer he waited, the more impatient he'd become until he challenged me outright. And he had no intention of letting me leave here without getting what he wanted. "Eat up, little girl," Dutch said, boisterously. "You're gonna need your strength." Then he barked out a laugh, like it was his own little private joke.

Rose didn't say a word, her expression blank. Only the slight tremor of her body gave away the effect Dutch had on her.

"Good girl," I murmured. "Finish your hot dog, and we'll go back to the cabin." She looked up at me with solemn eyes and gave an almost imperceptible shake of her head, not wanting the food. In that moment, I could cheerfully have throttled Dutch. I didn't need this. *Any* of this. "Go on," I encouraged her. "I swear I won't let him touch you, but you have to eat."

She nibbled on the rest of the hot dog, finishing all but the last bite. I popped it into my mouth, then stood, helping her to her feet as well. We had thirty minutes to get back and contact my team or they'd come in, guns blazing. I thought I could manage this but Sting had to know the complication I now had so he could inform Alexei. Or Azriel. 'Cause even I didn't have enough balls to tell Alexei I had his daughter inside this fucking compound. He'd put a bullet in my Goddamned head, and I wouldn't blame him. I thought back to everything I'd already done. Just kissing the girl was grounds for castration. Not only would he probably kill me, but it would put Iron Tzars in a bad light with Shadow Demons.

The really bad part -- as far as I was concerned -- was that I cared less about the effect on my club than I did about the effect on the tiny woman in my possession. Since I'd been a part of Iron Tzars, I'd never put anything above the club, but I was reevaluating that stance with this girl.

I led her back to the cabin and shut the door, locking us in. Not for the first time, I regretted not putting a better lock on the door. Hell, the cabin needed a new fucking door to be stronger. Or a whole new fucking cabin. Still, it would give me a few seconds if Bozz or Dutch decided to push the issue. A few seconds would be all I needed, but I still put a chair under the doorknob as one more thing. Fucking Christ, I didn't *fucking* need this!

The music still blared, and I was careful not to move into the line of sight of the camera Bozz had planted, but I didn't feel safe talking freely. Or maybe it was that I wanted to be close to Rose. I wanted to smell the clean, fresh scent of her hair as it tickled my nose when I spoke close to her ear. I wanted her in my arms as we pretended an intimacy I fucking craved. To say I wanted to fuck her was a gross understatement, but that wasn't happening.

I looked up to find her leaning against the small sink in the kitchen area, her arms wrapped around herself as she studied me from under her lashes. We stared at each other a long while. Then she started trembling and looked down at her feet.

Crossing the distance to her, I swore to myself as I grabbed her upper arm as gently as I could and took her to the bathroom. It was the one place inside this cabin I was sure wasn't bugged. I'd tested it on more than one occasion, pretending to talk to someone outside the compound and saying things I knew Dutch or Bozz would call me out on. Not enough to get me killed, but enough to rouse their suspicion and make them have to feel me out. I'd also swept it for bugs, same as I had in the main room. While the front room routinely had them, the bathroom hadn't had a listening device other than one I'd removed months ago, the first night I'd come to the compound. No one had said anything about it, so my guess was that the bathroom bug I'd removed in the bathroom either hadn't worked, or no one was monitoring it, and Bozz hadn't realized it was gone. Though Bozz was a son of a bitch, the man wasn't stupid, so I was betting my life they'd decided they trusted me at least enough to keep this one space free of listening devices.

Once we were inside and the door was shut, I framed her face with my hands, forcing her to look up at me. "You good, baby?"

She shook her head slightly, then her breath

started coming in shallow pants, tears springing to her eyes. One little sob let go before I pulled her into my arms and held her face against my chest while she had her meltdown.

It had to happen. No woman in her right mind wouldn't have been terrified by the situation Rose found herself in. I couldn't reassure her everything would be all right. There was a very high probability it wouldn't.

"I know, honey. I'm so sorry you're mixed up in this."

"Are they going to rape me?" Her question was so soft I nearly didn't catch it.

"Not as long as I live, Rose. I'll protect you with my last breath."

She looked up at me, tears flowing freely from frightened eyes. I swore. We had to have this talk, though after this minor meltdown, I was ready to say fuck it and call in the cavalry.

"I'm calling it. I won't risk you getting hurt. We'll figure something else out."

"Wait," she said softly, bunching her hand in my shirt. "How quickly can your team get here if we get into trouble?"

I tilted my head, trying to see where she was going with this. "At a moment's notice. I've got at least two guys on this place at all times. Right now, I've got ten members outside this compound ready to storm us in exactly fifteen minutes unless I call them off. If I give the word, they can come right now."

"Then wait." Rose still trembled in my arms, but her features hardened. "I don't want to leave anyone here. We get them all out, or we stay until we can."

There was no way to stop the growl of frustration. It was the plan I'd had all along, but seeing how terrified Rose was -- with good reason -- I'd changed my mind about keeping her with me. She needed to get to safety, and I was prepared to take the smaller victory. Then she had to go and volunteer to stay.

"You saw how everyone here is. If we stay, you're very much in danger. I'll protect you with my life, but it might not be enough. I'm only one guy. There are thirty-seven men in this compound who'd love to get their hands on you. Killin' me'd just be a bonus."

She straightened, lifting her chin in stubborn determination, even as her lower lip trembled slightly. "I'll do exactly what you tell me to. If at any time you feel the situation is getting out of hand, call in your club. I'm scared, but I can fight through it if it means we save innocents. It's what my dad would do."

"Honey, your dad would kill every motherfucking person in here, including me, if he knew you were here. I've got to tell my president so he can take the appropriate action to protect our club, but it's not going to make much difference. Once Alexei finds out you're here, it's over."

"Then don't tell him."

I had to really concentrate and replay her words in my head to believe she'd just suggested we not tell Alexei she was here. "Sting won't go for that. It'd bring the Shadow Demons down on our club like a plague. They'd kill everyone in the compound if something happened to you and we could have prevented it. Keepin' you here one fuckin' second longer than strictly necessary is not preventing it fast enough."

"Then I'll tell him myself. He'll send you anything you need to make this work as safely as possible."

OK, that got my attention. And sent my brain into overdrive. We'd never asked Shadow Demons for an assist. Yes, we worked for them so we could keep getting tech and weaponry from them, but we didn't work together. They gave us a task and we completed it. If they came in on this with us now, we might shut down the whole fucking outfit in this region.

What the *fuck* was I thinking?

"No. Out of the question. I should have already gotten you out of here, and that's what I'm gonna do now." I went to the water heater and got the sat phone. When I turned around, Rose was right behind me. She put her hand on my arm and reached for the phone, gently plucking it from me.

"This is Giovanni's."

"How do you know that?"

"Because I have one just like it. I left it turned off in my bedroom because I didn't want him and my dad monitoring every move I made. I wanted to live life on my own for a while. See what it was like outside that big mansion and the long arm of their protection."

"This isn't what you signed up for, Rose. It's the worst situation you could possibly be in."

"No, it's not. Though I won't deny it's close. I remember life before Mom and Alexei got together. We stayed in some pretty questionable places. Just the two of us. We had no one to turn to back then. Now, I have Alexei, Azriel, and Giovanni along with my mom and every single member of that household. The women here are in a much worse situation than I am. I have you to protect me. They have no one."

Without waiting for my consent, Rose punched in a number on the phone and put it on speaker.

"Atlas?" The man on the other end of the phone bit out my name, irritation in his voice.

"Gio?"

There was a pause. "Bella?"

"Yeah. It's me. Can you get Dad?"

"What are you doing calling from this number?" The anger and fear in Giovanni's voice told me the man knew exactly what was going on. He might not know the particulars, but the fact that Rose was anywhere near this fucking phone told him all he needed to know about the situation she was in.

"It's a long story, and we don't have that kind of time. I need you, Dad and Azriel to help the Iron Tzars. Right now."

I heard computer keys clicking in the background. "We're coming, sweetheart."

"Wait! No, Gio! They're trying to get a meet with --"

"I know who that fucker Dutch is trying to contact. I've been monitoring them since Sting put Atlas in there in the first place. You're not going to be in the same fucking state as the Swede, Bella. We're coming to get you."

"Gio, you have to let them do this." Her voice wavered. Rose was on the verge of tears again. "Please. Use all those things you make to figure out a way to keep me safe until they catch this guy. I don't want to die or be r-raped," she stumbled over the word and more tears overflowed her eyes, "but my life is not worth the lives of dozens of women and children. More if he's allowed to continue."

"Not going to happen."

"Gio, I could never live with myself --"

There was a scuffle in the background, then another voice interrupted me. "Bella? What's going on? Why are you in that fucking hell hole?"

"Daddy." Rose did let out a little sob then.

"Please, Daddy. They have to catch the Swede. I couldn't live with myself if he hurt so many others because they pulled me out and blew the chance."

"I'm not even entertaining the thought of you staying there, Bella. I don't give a fuck who else is in danger, you're my first priority."

Her voice changed from terrified girl to hardened warrior. Or, at least, a hardened warrior who was still scared of the battle to come. "I called to ask you to join the Iron Tzars in doing this. To help them catch this guy and kill the shit out of him. I swear I'll never ask you for anything else again as long as I live, but I *need you to do this*."

There was a scuffle and the sound of a glass crashing in the background. As well as some very inventive swearing.

"Bella, it's Azriel. Tell me the situation as you see it. Describe the area and the men. The fortifications." Azriel sounded better in control than Giovanni or Alexei. I could tell he was acting as the voice of reason here. Hopefully, he'd have her lay it all out, then point out the reasons she needed to let us get her out.

"I'm not sure how big the compound is, but it has a chain-link fence around it topped with razor wire. Atlas says there are thirty-seven men here. I counted thirty-three when we joined the group to eat. Of those thirty-three, maybe fifteen carried themselves like they'd be good in a fight. Half of those were drunk. The president, Dutch, isn't as smart as he thinks he is, but he's cunning. He likes to play his members off each other, but I'm pretty sure it's backfiring. Bozz, one of his inner circle is gunning for him, though he appears like he's solidly in Dutch's corner. He bugged our cabin with a tiny camera, but I watched him talking to another man when we ate and Dutch was talking with Atlas. If I read Bozz's lips correctly, Dutch doesn't know about the camera. Bozz isn't spying on Atlas so much as he's testing the camera out to see if Atlas finds it. He's wanting to put eyes on Dutch. Again, I'm not a hundred percent, but I think he's looking for the right time to kill Dutch."

There was silence so long I thought maybe we'd lost the connection. Might be just as well. I still wasn't certain how much I trusted the phone's connection not to be traced. Obviously, Giovanni believed his gadget was foolproof. And, Jesus fuck! How the fuck had Rose gotten all that information in her one outing?"

"You sure about all that?" I couldn't help but ask the question.

She shrugged, wiping tears from her cheek with one hand. "As sure as I can be given the brief time I had to watch. I did what you told me to, Atlas. Aside from the four men I didn't see, you're the deadliest man here. After you, Bozz and the man he was talking to. Dutch might lead these men, but probably only because he's killed a few so the rest fall in line." She ducked her head. "At least, that's my take on the situation. I only had an hour or so, and yeah. I was scared out of my mind. But I don't think I'm wrong."

"How'd you learn to do that?"

"My degree is in criminal psychology. I don't have much experience, but the main players in this case are textbook as far as I can see. Given more time, I can narrow down specific character traits and predict their actions. Dutch, in particular, is unstable. The thing that makes him dangerous is his mental instability. He's a psychopath. He'll carefully plot out any move he makes to get what he wants. He'll pretend to be your friend or to be on your side, but he's not. He's on his own side. The side that gets him the end result he's looking for. Right now, something is holding him in check. Probably the money he believes he'll make when he sells people to this Swede guy. He believes you give him the best chance to maximize his profits, so he'll back off you. For a while."

"Yeah, he said as much to Bozz when he told him to lay off the women."

"I think Bozz is a sociopath. He doesn't care about others, certainly not the women he hurts. He has outbursts of anger and rage over the slightest things. He'll rationalize his behavior, just like he did with you tonight. He said this was his club, and he'd do what he wanted. In his mind, because the women are in his home, he can do whatever he wants."

"So these are the people we're dealing with." Ariel's voice coming from the phone startled me. I'd forgotten about them, thinking the connection had been lost.

"The main players, yes," I confirmed. "I don't like this, Rose. I get where you're coming from, but I'm not willing to risk your life."

"You said you could keep me safe."

"And I believe I can. But I don't want to take that chance."

"You were willing before."

"I was willing to consider it before. Mainly because, at the time, I didn't have any options. Now I do."

"How much time do you have before Sting sends in his men?" Rose's eyes still glistened with tears, but there was a steely determination in her gaze that had me swearing on the inside. There was no way I was going to win this fight with her. I shrugged, not in any hurry to answer her. If I could wait just a little bit longer, Sting would take the decision out of my hands.

"Atlas…" Rose's expression hardened. She was still pale and trembling slightly, but this side of her was throwing me. It was… unexpected. And turning me the fuck on. "Tell me how much longer we have."

"Ten minutes."

"Giovanni --"

"No way, Rose."

Then she did something else I wasn't expecting. "Are you going to trust Sting and the others to take this place with me inside? Think of everything that could go wrong. Wouldn't you rather be in place to control the situation?"

There was another silence before Alexei could be heard in the background swearing and possibly destroying many expensive things. "Goddammit, Bella! I swear to God, you're gonna be the fucking death of me. Atlas, tell Sting to hold. We'll be there in three hours. You make sure you have a direct fucking line to him and his team, Atlas. Anything starts you can't control, call them in."

I gave Rose my best intimidating, pissed-as-hell stare. "I'll call him now."

Without further comment, the line really did disconnect this time. I immediately called Sting, never taking my gaze from Rose.

"Stand down, prez. Expect company in the form of the Shadow Demons."

"Are you fucking kidding me?"

"Nope. They'll fill you in on the development. Remember that problem I told you I had? They'll fill you in on her."

"Her." It wasn't a question.

"Yep."

"Well, trouble always starts with a woman. Why the fuck would this be any different?" After that last disgruntled comment, Sting disconnected, and I put the phone back in its hiding place.

"I swear to God, when this is over, I'm gonna beat your ass, girl."

Chapter Four
Bellarose

Once business was done, there was nothing to do but wait. "This whole fucking affair has been nothing but waiting." Atlas muttered his disgruntlement as we exited the bathroom. "It's after midnight. Since we're not at the party, we need to act like we're going to bed."

I nodded. He turned off the music before moving closer to the bed and beckoning me to him. He whipped his shirt over his head and tossed it to the chair where Bozz had planted the camera, then did the same with my shirt. I was so surprised all I could do was gasp. When I went to cover myself, he shook his head as he stripped off his jeans and tossed them too.

Shivering, I followed suit, though he took my jeans from me to do the tossing. I knew he was trying to cover the camera without trying to look like he was trying to cover the camera, so I didn't protest.

I stood before him in nothing but my underwear. I was highly conscious of my semi-naked state, but also of his. And, I had to face it, the man looked far better naked than I did. Had the situation not been what it was, Atlas was a man I'd be panting after. Tattoos covered his arms and chest. Muscles played with every movement. A light dusting of hair spread from that wide chest, tapering off to a goodie trail leading beneath his boxer briefs. He was as mouthwatering as he was dangerous.

He winced and shook his head slightly. Yeah. I knew what was next. I might sleep in my panties, but definitely not my bra. Acutely aware of the fact that there could be people watching, I took a breath before unfastening my bra and letting it slide down my arms.

With a brief glance at Atlas, I handed the flimsy lace garment to him, and he chucked it like he had the other things.

I wasn't sure I could keep my composure if he found me lacking. Which was entirely possible. I was a nerd. Not an athlete. Though my dad made sure I didn't take my studies too seriously and made me get up and move, I hated exercise. I wasn't fat, but I definitely had extra flesh, which included big boobs, hips, and thighs. Not to mention the little stomach pooch I'd sprouted the last few months.

The deep growl coming from him startled me. One look at the hunger in his eyes, and I knew I was in trouble. Mainly because I was certain that look mirrored the one in my own eyes. I'd had one lover in my life, and the sex had been tepid at best. I knew from the kisses Atlas and I had shared that sex with him would be *scalding*.

But we weren't doing that. We'd probably share a few more kisses, and we'd certainly share the same bed, but sex was a line neither of us would cross. I'd probably never see Atlas again after this was over, thank God. Because I was certain I'd never be able to look at him without remembering those kisses. I found myself wanting a few more, no matter how inappropriate. Besides, it kept my mind from going places that would have me backing out of this and calling in my dad and Atlas's club.

Atlas leaned in close so his lips were right against my ear, his arms going around me. "I swear I won't hurt you, Rose." His rough murmur was like an erotic stroke of his hand. "We have to sleep in the same bed. I have to hold you. But I swear that's as far as it goes. If I didn't get that camera covered and Dutch or Bozz came in here with me on the couch…"

"I know." I made sure to keep him between me and the other part of the house, my voice no more than a whisper.

"You can tell me to back off."

"No." I stepped into his embrace and rested my cheek against his wide chest. "It's OK. Really. We can't risk…"

"I know." He stepped back and scrubbed a hand over his face. "Fuck."

I turned and climbed into the small bed and pulled the covers over me, lying on my side facing away from him. He was silent for the longest time, then he sighed, and the bed dipped behind me. Atlas moved me so that my head was pillowed on his arm, and he wrapped me up tightly against his body. I couldn't help the sigh of pleasure. This wasn't something I'd ever experienced. Even the one guy I'd had sex with hadn't actually slept with me.

"You good?" As always, his voice was right beside my ear. He nuzzled my neck gently, and I had to wonder if it was a move to gentle me or if it was simply a habit he had. Was this how he treated all his lovers?

I nodded. "Yes," I breathed.

"Fuck." He tightened his grip on me, biting out the word viciously. I knew what the problem was but was afraid to tell him it was all right in case we were heard. We'd already said too much without the cover of music. Nestled between the cheeks of my ass, Atlas's cock pulsed almost violently. I knew I should be embarrassed or outraged, but even though I was in this situation -- maybe even because of it -- I couldn't muster the effort. In fact, it fueled my own lust because, I had to face it, Atlas was everything I'd ever wanted in a man. At least, I thought he was. Outside of all this, I had no idea how he'd be with me. Just because I gave him a hard-on after seeing my tits and us being mashed so close together in this tiny bed, didn't mean I was his type. I seriously doubted a man like him looked at me twice under normal circumstances.

"Just a few more hours, baby." His whisper was right at my ear. I turned my head to look back at him, shaking it slightly. He groaned before nipping the side of my neck, causing me to yelp. "Not talkin' 'bout that with you." There was an edge to his whisper now.

I turned over and pulled him close so I could put my lips next to his ear. "You know we need to stay and stop this guy." I was careful to speak so softly it would only carry to him and not any listening devices. At least, I hoped I did.

"You'll do what I tell you to," he growled.

Again, I shook my head, lifting my chin stubbornly.

"You know the decision has pretty much been taken from you, right?" He cupped my chin in his big hand, his thumb and fingers pressing into my jaw. It wasn't painful, but enough I knew he meant business. He was being as careful as I was not to say something that could get us both in trouble, but I understood exactly what he meant. Dad said he'd be here in three hours. Which meant, exactly three hours and two minutes later, he'd come in guns blazing.

We stared at each other for a long moment. It was dark, but the moonlight filtering through the dirty window was enough to let me see his face clearly. My lips parted, and I sucked in a breath. This man was so potent he made me forget every good sense I had. In that moment, all I wanted was for him to kiss me and take me away from this awful place to a world of sensual pleasure.

His hand moved around to snatch a handful of my hair, yanking my head back. "Don't fuckin' look at me like that, girl. I will fuckin' eat you alive."

"Yes… Please." The little plea escaped before I could censor myself, because I needed to give him anything he wanted. If I continued to let my guard down around him, to let temptation rule me, I'd give myself to him and damn the consequences.

"Goddammit," he swore. Then he took my mouth in a kiss that put the other kisses we'd shared to shame.

With a wicked thrust of his tongue, Atlas bullied his way inside my mouth, demanding I give him everything. The second I surrendered to him, he shifted his grip on me, wrapping his other arm around me from beneath to grip my hair in that hand while the other one urged my leg high over his hip.

"This what you're gunnin' for, girl? You wantin' a hard ride?" I shook my head slightly. "Don't lie to me!"

"I don't… I don't know."

"I think you do."

"I just… I want this before… I mean, if this is the last day…"

"It ain't gonna be." His gruff declaration sounded more like an order than anything reassuring.

"I don't want to not have this, Atlas. Please."

He pulled me tighter against him so his cock rubbed between my legs directly over my clit. I couldn't help but cry out. Instantly he covered my mouth with his again, swallowing my screams.

"Fuck me," he hissed. "You're so fuckin' turned-on you're about to blow. Aren't you?"

Was I? I thought I might be. Thankfully, he

didn't require an answer. Just kept kissing me, thrusting his tongue deeply and aggressively. I gave a tentative stroke of my own, trying to follow his lead. I had no idea why I needed this, but I did. Even knowing I'd regret it later.

Atlas rocked against me, putting the most delicious friction on my clit as he continued to kiss me. Whimpers escaped along with little sighs I had no hope of preventing. Thankfully, Atlas was in more control than I was because all I could do was follow his lead and just... *feel*.

I knew this was a bad idea. Normally, I'd have never acted like this. Even with the one lover I'd had, the need to come had never ridden me this hard. Maybe it was the danger we were in. Maybe it was the man. Or a combination of both. All I knew was I'd decided I wanted all I could get with Atlas. If that was one orgasm or twenty, I wanted it with everything in my being.

* * *

Atlas

I was going to hell, and Alexei Petrov was going to send me there. When it happened, I wouldn't lift a finger to defend myself. I'd go willingly, knowing I'd had the most luscious, delicious, passionate woman I'd ever encountered. In any other situation, I'd take her as high as she wanted to go before flashing a cocky grin as I walked away from her.

Not like this, though. I had to keep her close and found my grip on her was tightening with every fucking second that passed. She shouldn't be here. What's more, she should be begging her daddy to get her the fuck out. Not my little Rose, though. And for the right reasons, too. She was as determined as I was to see this thing through. Only, I wasn't so sure I was as committed as I was when I'd met her. I wasn't sure I really gave a damn about anything other than getting this woman to safety.

Unfortunately, my cock cared about something else. Which wasn't happening. Didn't mean I couldn't make her come, though. I knew this feeling well, though, with a beautiful, courageous woman in my arms, I admit I'd never felt lust as strong as I did right now. We might die tonight or tomorrow. It was all too easy to want to take comfort in each other.

I stopped kissing her long enough to look down into her lovely face. She was definitely with me in the moment. Her eyes gleamed, and her lips were parted, kiss-swollen from me. I had no idea how much experience she had, but I was betting way the fuck less than me. Which meant I had to be careful.

"You realize you're feeling this way because of the situation, right? You're scared, and I'm your safety net."

She nodded before thrusting her hips at me as she bit down on her bottom lip. I got the message. She knew but didn't fucking care.

"I ain't gonna fuck you, Rose. Your daddy'd kill me, and I'd deserve it. He'll likely kill me just for kissin' you. But I'm gonna give you the relief you need, then we're both gonna rest for the next couple of hours." I was careful to whisper and only right next to her ear or her lips. "This is gonna be tricky, and you have to know we probably have an audience. Either watchin' or listenin'." She nodded. With my face against hers, I could feel her cheeks heat in embarrassment. "That a hard no?" She shook her head, tightening her legs around my waist.

"All right, then. You keep silent except to scream

your pleasure. When you come, I want to hear it." Her eyes widened, and she shook her head. I smacked the outside of her thigh. "You'll scream my name when you fuckin' come, girl. Get me?" For emphasis, I thrust my cock against her, scraping over her clit through my boxers and her panties. This time, she cried out before snapping her mouth shut. She glared at me, baring her teeth. "That's it. You give me your pleasure. Don't say a word otherwise. The only sound you're allowed to make is when you come."

I leaned down to take one nipple into my mouth. I shouldn't do this, but I couldn't help myself. I had to taste her. It was a compulsion I should have wanted to stop, but knew I wouldn't. This would likely be the only time I ever got the chance to sample her passion, and I was grabbing it with both hands. Later I'd beat myself up. She wanted this as much as I did, so I was going to give it to us both.

I slid my way down her body, nipping at her skin as I went. The little whimpers coming from her were sweet music, but I didn't want that. I wanted her silent until she came.

"Hush or I stop." Like that was fucking happening.

Immediately, she slapped a hand over her mouth, and I chuckled. As I continued down her body, I inhaled deeply, needing to take her scent inside me. To keep it there so I never forgot. This would probably be the only time I ever got this close to her, and I had a primal need to keep her scent inside me where I could take it out and remember.

I was a jaded man. I'd had women from all walks of life in all parts of the world. None of them had ever stirred me the way Rose did. She was beautiful and so fucking smart and brave it fucking scared me, but I wanted her with a passion that bordered on obsession.

I stripped off her panties, and the second I reached her bare mound, I found myself trembling with need. I wrapped my arms around her thighs to hold her open. Her breath came in short, quick pants. She tilted her pelvis up at me when I paused.

In the moonlight, her sex glistened with moisture, her arousal clear. "Fuckin' wet." I looked up at her. She braced herself on one elbow, still covering her mouth with her hand. "Not a sound until you come, pet. Not. One. Sound."

She nodded, and I dug in.

The second my tongue touched her clit, Rose let out a shrill, anguished scream. At first I was afraid I'd hurt her or that she was afraid or had changed her mind. Then I realized her pussy had gushed with the explosion within her. She thrashed her head from side to side, raising her knees high and spreading her thighs.

And I… was… *lost*!

* * *

Rose

I know what Atlas said, but I needed more than a one-sided interaction. I wanted him. Atlas. I had no idea what he did in his club or for a living, but I wanted every second I could get with him. I knew this could never last beyond these walls, and I had no desire to stay here a moment longer than necessary, but I wanted Atlas for my own. Since I couldn't have that, I was going to have him now. *Better to have loved and lost than never to have loved at all.* Right?

The second time I came, I gripped his hair in a tight hold and ground his face against me. Atlas growled and snarled, slapping the side of my ass before sliding his hands under me, gripping the fleshy globes and holding my pussy to his mouth as if they were fused together. My screams grew louder and louder until I *wailed* his name at the top of my lungs. I'd be surprised if they didn't hear me at the clubhouse.

"Fuck! That's it, baby. Keep comin'!" He swatted my ass again, nipping at my lower lips before sucking my clit once more.

I did. My body spasmed, and I was barely able to suck in a breath before another scream was torn from me. Fingers tightening in his hair, I pulled him up my body with a vicious yank. Atlas swore, but it didn't seem like it was in pain. And, honestly, I figured if the pain enhanced my pleasure, it probably did the same for him. Given the situation we found ourselves in, I was sure he fed off the small amount of violence and the pain. I pulled at his boxers until he dropped them to the floor. When I had him over top of me, between my legs, I pulled him down for a kiss filled with as much hunger and desperation as I could. This was happening.

Atlas bit down on my lip, and I gasped in pain and surprise. "Aggressive little vixen. You're not leadin' this dance. I'm in control."

I nodded as I ground my pussy against his dick, getting it wet with my juices.

"Fuckin' little witch! Move on me!" Atlas looked almost feral as I did as he asked, tilting my hips up and down, my ankles locked around his waist, my legs holding him as tightly as I could. His movements were hard as he thrust against me, rubbing his dick over my clit with every thrust. I obeyed his command, but when he started to move with me, I moved just that little bit quicker than I should have. My move made sure his dick was aimed straight at my pussy. One hard shove -- one he'd meant to rub against my clit -- and he impaled me in one smooth glide.

"What the fuck?" Atlas jerked in surprise, his eyes filled with hunger and shock. "Goddamned fuckin' little witch!" He looked like he couldn't decide if he wanted to throw me off him or roll us over and fuck me hard, fast, and brutally. He yelled, the veins standing out on his neck as he held himself still buried deep inside me.

"Atlas!"

"Fuck! Fuck! FUCK!"

I screamed again. My hands flew to his ass, griping and digging my nails into his flesh. "Fuck me," I gasped. "Please, Atlas… Please…" My pleas were whispered, even though he'd told me not to say anything, not to make a sound unless I was coming. It was asking for trouble, but I could no more have stopped the words than I could have stopped breathing.

"Goddamn. Motherfuck!"

Atlas shuddered once. Twice. Then he started riding me hard and fast. A teeth-clattering ride. His thrusts scraped over my clit in a frantic rhythm and, with the knowledge that Atlas was inside me, the fullness of him pulsing and throbbing, I came with one final scream. Atlas bellowed, sounding like he was charging into battle. I felt his cum emptying into me as his cock pulsed angrily.

"Fuckin' little witch…" His words were harsh, but his tone soft. Like he was dazed. Confused. He shuddered once more, grinding himself against me so that he was as deep as he could go, and held himself there. A satisfied growl rumbled deliciously in his chest, vibrating against me where we were mashed together. "What the fuck have you done?" Instead of taking out his anger on me, Atlas nuzzled my neck, kissing and sucking lightly before finding my lips again. The tenderness in his kiss nearly made tears come to my eyes. It felt like praise for my body's acceptance of his, but that was ludicrous. He was probably still in a state of shock.

When he pulled back to look at me, there was a hard determination in his gaze. He didn't say anything right away, but stroked damp hair away from my forehead. Then he shook his head, his lips turning up in a kind of dismay. "Fuckin' little witch…" It seemed like he was stuck on that phrase to describe me. The way he said it, though, made me think that maybe he wasn't angry with me. I wasn't sure.

I nodded, afraid to say anything. Not only because we might be bugged, but because I had no idea what Atlas was thinking. Saying something might push him over the edge.

He sighed, then pushed himself up, taking me with him. Urging me to keep my legs wrapped around him, he carried me to the bathroom and set me on my feet before shutting the door and locking it.

For long moments, Atlas stood at the door before groaning softly and leaning his head against the plywood. "I'm a dead man."

Again, I was afraid to say anything. I knew what I'd done. Atlas had every right to be furious at me, and I couldn't defend myself. What could I say? "Sorry" didn't seem to cut it. I'd taken what he hadn't offered. Something he hadn't been prepared to give me.

I backed away from him, putting my back against the wall, my hands behind me. When he turned around, I expected to see anger. Maybe even betrayal. Hadn't I basically just… raped him? The man was close to three times my size. He was big and strong and could have easily shoved away from me if he'd wanted to. Right?

"Don't look at me like you're afraid I'm gonna hurt you." Atlas shook his head, closing his eyes briefly. "You good?"

I nodded. Was I? I'd just had the most fantastic sex I'd ever dreamed of -- the stuff of fantasies. I was good, but I was ashamed. Ducking my head, I sighed softly.

"Come here, baby." Atlas took my arm and tugged me to him. His arms came around me tightly, a secure hold that seemed to completely enclose me. "It'll be all right. You're good. I'm here, and I'm not lettin' anything happen to you."

Surprised, I looked up at him. "Why are you worried about me? I... I *forced* you to..." I spoke softly, aware that even though the bathroom seemed to be the one place Atlas felt comfortable talking, I still had to be careful.

"You did it because you're scared. You're living in the moment in case you don't have many more. I get it. I feel it too. Your daddy'll be here soon, and we can get the fuck outta here. Then everything will be all right."

"Not without the other girls. *And* unless we can take care of the Swede, or whoever he is. I don't want to leave anyone behind, and I don't want all the time you've spent here to be in vain. We're going to save everyone we can who would be affected by him, and then he's gonna die."

"God, you're fierce." Threading his fingers through my hair once more, Atlas kissed me. There was still that biting hunger, but it was tempered. "You'll make a fine ol' lady. I'll be proud to have you."

I sucked in a breath. "You'd do that?"

"What? Make you my woman? Honey, I was already fightin' it. With this?" He waved his hand to indicate me and him together. "I want you with me. So, I'm all yours."

"You don't have to do that."

"Tell me something, baby. You on birth control?"

I blinked up at him. "Uh..."

"Uh-huh. That's what I thought." He shook his head. "Ain't takin' a chance with you. There's a possibility you could be carryin' my kid. I'll be there to protect you both."

A sting of hurt stabbed me. "You don't have to. I'm perfectly capable of taking care of myself and anyone else who comes along. Even if I couldn't, my mom and dad would help me. I've got a strong support system. I'm not going to trap you in a loveless relationship. Because, if you went to another woman, not only would you break my heart, my daddy'd kill you."

"Well aware of that." He chuckled. "He'll likely kill me anyway, but in any event, I don't share. I don't expect you to, either. Tell you what. We'll table this discussion until we're safely out of here. Good?"

"Yeah. I can accept that."

Chapter Five

Atlas

An hour later, I contacted Sting. The Shadow Demons had arrived with a tactical unit, a helicopter, and more firepower than most small countries. They were confident that they could kill everyone in the place that needed killing and bring out everyone else. Sting didn't say whether or not Alexei included me in with the people who'd be coming out or the ones who needed killing. If he knew what I'd done to his daughter an hour earlier, I'd definitely be with the latter.

Of all the fucking things. Rose had gotten one over on me. Big time. She either felt guilty about it now or was regretting it, but done was done. Anytime I reached for her, she came willingly, letting me hold her. I thought I needed it as much as she did. She'd gotten her momentary fix, but she'd also given herself something else to worry about.

Later. I'd figure it out later. One thing at a time.

"We're ready to come in. Just waiting on the word from Giovanni that everything is clear. He's working on hacking into the club's security. As well as every phone, smart TV, computer, and anything else hooked up to the Internet or a cell tower. Said you had your place covered as well, though he didn't seem happy about it. Not sure what's up with that." Right. I'd just bet he wasn't. Which told me where I stood with Alexei. What Giovanni knew, Alexei knew. And if Giovanni had hacked into my security setup already, he knew what had happened with me and Rose.

"Good. Anytime you want to do this, let me know. I'll make sure Rose gets through it in one piece."

"You watch yourself too, Atlas. Don't plan on

losin' you in this shithole."

"Just so you know, she's trying to fight me on it. She's insisting I complete my mission here and take out not only every motherfucker in this club, but that Swede person as well. She's not wavered from that demand. I'm done, though. It's not worth it to risk her life."

There was a silence. "What's goin' on, Atlas? Has something happened?"

My president knew me very well. "You could say that. I'll give you three guesses what, but you'll only need one. So my life's forfeit no matter what. I accept that. But you have to promise to keep an eye on Rose. Make sure she's protected. Even if she's locked away in that mansion they call a fuckin' clubhouse. Find a way."

"Sweet Jesus, Atlas. Couldn't you have picked a different woman to rescue on the side of the fuckin' road? Christ!" There was a heavy sigh on the other end. I could almost see Sting digging into his eyes with his thumb and fingers as he tried to hold on to his temper. "We'll worry about that later. Right now, just lay low. It's nearly dawn. Alexei will probably want to go soon."

"Keep me updated so there's no surprises. I don't want to accidentally shoot someone I shouldn't."

"I'll keep that in mind."

Once out of the bathroom, I went to Rose. Again, she welcomed me, folding herself into my arms like she fucking belonged there. I scooped her up and took her to the bed. I laid her down and crawled on top of her, wedging my hips between her thighs. We were both still naked, so my cock wanted to head to the promised land once more. I settled for rubbing myself over her clit in a lazy glide.

"How you feelin'? Still OK?" She nodded, looking up into my eyes with a tentative smile. I leaned down to kiss her sweet lips because I couldn't help myself.

Rose's legs wrapped around my hips and she gave a soft groan of pleasure. Her hips tilted to mine, much like they had before. This time, though, I knew I'd be the one to slip inside her. The damage was done and, now that the idea had taken hold, I wasn't as opposed to the thought of her carrying my kid as I should have been.

"I love how you feel against me, Rose. And you're so fuckin' beautiful it hurts." I whispered the words at her ear. When she shivered against me and whimpered, I had to smile. "I think my girl is greedy for my cock. Yes?"

She nodded and squeezed her legs tighter around me. I wanted nothing more than to lose myself in her body. I couldn't do that, but I could bring her another orgasm. And fill her with more cum.

I pressed the head of my cock against her entrance, then stopped and pulled back to look at her as I stroked her hair away from her face. The silky strands were still damp from our earlier round, and I couldn't help the surge of masculine pride that I'd taken her that far. I raised an eyebrow at her, asking permission to slide inside her. She nodded her head even as she thrust her hips at me.

I waited until she settled somewhat before sliding inside her with a lazy roll of my hips. Even though I'd just fucked her, she was tight and gripping, still slick from her own arousal and my cum. Wrapping my arms around her, I continued the slow, lazy glide. There was no hurry at the moment, and I wanted to take my time. To bring her up gently before letting her crest over the edge.

My mouth found the pulse at her neck, and I sucked gently, marking her in the only way I could right now. When I got us back to the Iron Tzars compound, I'd get her a property patch and help her design her tattoo. Then she'd be mine, and there'd be nothing her daddy could do to prevent it. And I was sure he'd try. I was sixteen years her senior. I also wasn't a good man. No doubt her father wanted her to marry someone who'd killed a bit less than I had. Not to mention I had no idea how to run in the circles Petrov and his associates did. No. I wasn't good enough for Rose, and I knew it. Didn't change the fact that I was going to secure her for my own as quickly as possible.

Her pussy gripped me, and she gasped. I brought my mouth back to hers, kissing her as she found her release. The second she clamped down on me, Rose bit my lip, squeezing her eyes shut. A ragged grunt escaped her, and her pussy flooded my dick with her release. That was my cue to let myself go. I shuddered over her, my cock emptying in a scorching climax. Rose whimpered under me, still clutching my body with her arms and legs. Both of us were breathing hard. She didn't make a sound other than the occasional whimper or sigh.

"What the fuck am I gonna do with you, my beautiful little witch?" It was a question I had no idea how to answer. I knew what I wanted to do, but I wasn't sure how long I'd be alive after this job was done. Alexei was likely planning my death even now. If I had my way, though, I'd do what I promised. Patch her. Ink her. Make her my ol' lady.

I had leaned down to kiss her once more when there was a heavy pounding at the door. "What the fuck now?" I was pretty sure it was either Dutch or Bozz outside. Maybe some of their goons, but I didn't think so. At least, they wouldn't send other club members without one of them being present. Mainly because they knew I could give two fucks about anyone else in the club and damned sure wouldn't take orders from any of them.

"It's Bozz, Atlas. Open the fuck up before I break the fuckin' door in."

"I'm gonna kill that motherfucker." Instead of putting clothes on, I snagged my sidearm, checked the clip and chambered a round before stalking to the door and throwing it open. I brought up my gun to rest the barrel against Bozz's forehead, cocking it. "You've got five seconds to tell me what's so fuckin' important. Then I kill you."

Bozz's eyes got wide, and he backed up a step, hands raised. "Easy, man. Dutch wants you. Said I was to stay behind to protect your woman." He grinned at the last like he was looking forward to that particular task.

I didn't acknowledge him with an answer, just slammed the door in his face. To his credit, Bozz didn't barge his way inside, though I did hear him chuckle behind the door. Fucker wasn't as stupid as he looked.

"Get dressed, Rose."

She hurried to do as I asked. Both of us were ready to go in less than five minutes. I snagged my phone off the charger, made sure it was on, then stuck it in my back pocket. "You stay at my side at all times. Put your hand in the waist of my jeans or my back pocket. I won't be holding your hand, because I'll need mine both free in case I need to defend us. No matter what, you stay near me, and whatever you do, don't make a sound. You got me? Not even a whimper.

Understand?"

She nodded, and I took her hand, guiding it to my back. She dug her fingers into the waist and gripped the fabric. I looked back at her, and she nodded at me, a look of raw determination on her face.

Opening the door, I scowled at Bozz. "Lead the way." I had my gun in my hand. My finger was no longer on the trigger, and it was no longer cocked, but I wasn't leaving it behind and risk being caught unarmed when we went to the clubhouse. I had no doubt that was where we were going.

Once inside, the noise and sensory overload of the raucous party was enough to distract anyone. I could almost feel Rose cringing behind me, but she kept her hand firmly in the waist of my jeans. My gaze constantly shifted to the men and women in the room. No one seemed to pay us any attention as the party raged on. The place smelled of booze, pot, sex, and sweat. Not normally a combination that would bother me, but after having my nose buried in the sweet skin of Rose's neck, not a scent I wanted invading the peace I'd found.

Bozz led us to Dutch's office. It was the one place in the compound I hadn't bugged. I wanted him to think it was the one place he was safe, if he ever found the other bugs. Giovanni had tapped into my phone so another bug wasn't needed, though I'd have felt better if I had planted one in here. I had the feeling Sting was going to need to send everyone in sooner rather than later. There was something just that little bit off about Dutch tonight. The man sat behind his desk, his feet propped up, hands behind his head. "Atlas! Come in! Come in!"

"There some fuckin' reason you dragged me and my woman in here tonight?"

"Just invitin' you to the party, man. Relax. Do a few lines or a joint. Got plenty of drugs and women to go around."

"I don't mingle with your club, Dutch. I came here to do a job, and that's what I'm doin'."

"Yeah? Since you got here I've killed eight club members and lost several brats I was gonna sell. Tell me how you're helpin' me. Huh?"

"The eight men you killed were undercuttin' you. Tryin' to take over the club in a very permanent way. As to the kids, I wasn't the one guardin' them." I glanced at Bozz, who growled, his hands closing into fists at his side.

Dutch's gaze turned to Bozz, and the president looked uncertain before he grunted and stood. "So you weren't." He pulled a weapon from behind his back and shot Bozz in the head before turning the gun on me. "Tell me why I shouldn't kill you and take your little whore for myself."

"As high as you are, I doubt you could do much with her. You can try to kill me, but even with the weapon already in your hand, the odds of you coming out of that confrontation alive are slim to none." I wasn't worried for myself. I could easily take out this guy if I had to. The only question was, could I do it and not risk Rose getting hurt or killed?

Dutch and I stared at each other, neither giving an inch. Then Dutch lowered his weapon, laughing evilly. "You're a good soldier, Atlas. I knew it from the second you rode into this compound. I want you in this club as the new Sergeant at Arms."

"I have my own club. And I ain't patchin' over. I'm here to do a job. Nothin' more."

"You don't seem to understand. I'm not askin' you if you want the job. I'm tellin' you, you got it."

Several men filed into the office. Two of them dragged out the remains of Bozz and shoved him out the door before closing it behind them. Four other men dragged in a short table with metal loops on either side and leather straps at either end and the middle. It was solid, like a giant brick. My gut tightened. Something was off. Then another man entered with what looked like a branding iron and a five-gallon propane tank attached to a torch. That sickening feeling in my gut got worse.

It took a moment for the reality of what was happening to fully sink in. That moment's hesitation cost me. Before I could bring my weapon to bear on Dutch, I was disarmed and restrained by the remaining four men. I felt Rose's grip being ripped from me, but she didn't cry out or make any other sound. There was a scuffle and the sound of flesh hitting flesh. Probably one of the bastards hitting her.

Rage filled me. I roared my protest, fighting with all I had. Two more men came to assist the four already on me. I managed to get turned around where I could see Rose. She staggered after the blow, looking dazed. She shook her head and looked around her until she saw me. Our gazes met and clung to each other.

"Bind him and strip her." Dutch barked out the command. Again, Rose fought. I did too, but the four men had me secured while the other two helped with Rose. When they finished, her clothes had been ripped from her body, and two of the men held her by her upper arms. Rose didn't say a word through the whole thing. It felt like zip ties at my wrists, but I couldn't be sure.

"Kneel, Atlas." Dutch grinned, like he had the upper hand and he knew it. I knew what was about to happen, and there was no way I survived it.

Instead of kneeling, I spat in Dutch's direction. "When this is over, you're gonna die. It won't be quick."

"You're assuming you'll still be living. No one leaves this club. You live and die here. You don't want to be Sergeant at Arms? I have no other use for you." When the four men tried to shove me to my knees, I fought. I landed kicks to one of them, but another man managed to punt me behind the knees, and I went down hard. My gaze went back to Rose. She looked terrified, but had her lips firmly closed. Her chin quivered, but her eyes stayed on me as she watched them kick me once I was down.

"That's for the kick you landed," one of them bit out.

Once they had me on my knees, they looped something around my arms and secured me to the floor with my hands behind my back. I tested the tie but there was no give. I was well and truly caught. Thankfully, no one had thought to search me. If they had, someone might have taken the phone in my back pocket. I was surprised they hadn't noticed it when they secured my hands to the floor.

Dutch nodded to the men holding Rose. They dragged her over to the table and bent her over it, securing her wrists and ankles to the rings. She struggled but was no match for the size and strength of the two men manhandling her. When they were done, she lay with her upper body on the table, her toes barely touching the floor. Her legs were spread, giving anyone in the room access to her if they wanted it. And it was likely that was coming if Alexei and Sting didn't get here quickly.

Her wrists were secured with her arms down toward the floor, stretched tightly so there was no give to the leather straps that secured her. They also put a leather strap over her back, just below her shoulders and secured so tightly it dented her skin. One man held her head still, turning it so she faced me. Then they fastened a strap through smaller loops in the side of the table, the strap wrapping over her head so the side of her face lay on the surface. She was held immobile. Theirs to do with as they wished. And there was absolutely nothing I could do about it.

Continuing to struggle, trying to find just that little bit of give to the restraints holding me, I hoped with all my heart Giovanni was listening through the connection he had with my phone. They'd unleash hell once they figured out we needed help.

"You're a fuckin' dead man, Dutch."

He grinned. "It's not me who's bound and on his knees, Atlas. You act so high and mighty. Like you're king of all you survey." He sneered at me. "Let me tell you what's going to happen." He circled the table where Rose lay. Rose's gaze clung to mine. There was fear there, but also a steely determination. It was a good thing too, because she'd need every ounce she possessed to make it through this. "I'm gonna brand your woman. Like we would have done if you'd accepted my offer of being an officer in Soul Reapers. It will say 'Property of Atlas'." To prove to me this was going to happen, he took the branding iron from where one of his goons had set it up to heat when they'd first brought it to the room.

The brand Dutch picked up and showed me was exactly the way he'd described. The letters on the top formed the rocker, "Property of." The bottom spelled out my name, the type set replaceable with the desired name.

"Once she's branded, everyone who sees it will

know the bitch belonged to you. When they see me fuckin' her, they'll know I was the son of a bitch with balls big enough to take her from you. Every brother who fucks her will see that brand and know I took her from the biggest badass of them all." He got right up in my face then, baring his teeth with every word. "And they. Will. Fear. Me." We stared at each other, each of us hating the other.

When Dutch stood, he handed the branding iron back for his man to put it back in the flame. Then he turned to Rose. "Well, bitch. This is your time. Feel free to scream all you want. I know Atlas forbids it, but you're going to be mine soon, and I love the sound of women's screams. Only I like them to scream in pain. Something you're about to find out."

Rose's frightened, wide-eyed gaze clung to mine. I'd never felt more powerless in my life. Never *been* so powerless! Dutch moved out of her line of sight and she tried to follow him with her eyes. No doubt not wanting what was coming to sneak up on her. This was way more than she'd signed up for. And I'd failed her. I'd let her down. We'd walked straight into danger without even questioning it. Every single bit of this was on me.

"Rose! Eyes on me!" I snapped my command, expecting to get a beat down. Surprisingly, the men around me only chuckled, obviously not considering me a threat now that they had me on my knees on the floor. "You keep your focus on me. *Do not* look away." She tried to nod but couldn't move her head. So she blinked at me, the muscles in her jaw tightening as she gritted her teeth together.

The moment seemed to stretch on forever. Her frightened gaze focused securely on me. I saw one tear leak from the corner of her eye and trickle over the bridge of her nose. Then the fear changed to resignation, then hardened to fierce determination. I knew my woman had a spine of steel, but there was no way to fight this. The pain she was about to feel would break her.

Dutch chuckled as he picked up the iron once more. He waved it in the air over her back. To her credit, Rose didn't flinch. She kept her eyes fixed firmly on me. Her hands were in fists, and she fought to twist them free to no avail.

"Oh, to mark this lovely skin..." Dutch looked and sounded like a crazy man. There was a maniacal gleam in his eyes, a combination of his personality and whatever drugs he'd taken. "You will be my greatest masterpiece, my lovely little bitch." He leaned over her, kissing her cheek tenderly. "I look forward to seeing this brand on your skin. Even if it has that bastard's name on it. I was the man to take you from him. Never forget that. You'll be my whore. You'll obey me as thoroughly as you obeyed him."

Then he stepped back and, without further warning, pressed the iron to the skin of her shoulder blade. The sizzle and stench as her flesh burned made me want to puke. Not because I had a weak stomach, but because this was Rose! She was a woman who deserved gentle and tender. All I'd managed to bring her was pain.

I roared, doing my best to break the hold these men had on me. Whatever they had used to secure me to the floor snapped, and I struggled to my feet. I lashed out with everything in me, doing my best to fight them off long enough to get leverage to break the zip tie still around my wrists. I'm not sure how I managed it, but one second my hands were bound behind me, the next I'd broken them free. Then I

Bellarose

The pain was indescribable. Never had something hurt so fucking bad. But I kept my jaw clenched. Instead of keeping my gaze on Atlas, though, I shut my eyes tightly against the pain. Somehow, shutting out the sights around me helped me keep in any sound that wanted to break free. My jaw hurt, and my teeth felt like they were going to splinter with the pressure. The fiery brand on my shoulder faded quickly as the nerves deadened where it seared my skin.

I was aware of a struggle going on around me but couldn't open my eyes to see in case it ripped off the Band-Aid I had holding my control together. Atlas said I wasn't to make a sound, and I wouldn't. Not a cry. Not a whimper. I would be silent because it was what he told me to do.

Time meant nothing as I breathed through the pain and shock of what was happening. I fully expected Dutch would rape me in front of Atlas to torture him. I'd seen it before. One Alpha who'd bested another and wanted to flaunt the victory. With Atlas refusing to discuss sharing me with Dutch -- or any other member of this club -- Dutch would want to prove to Atlas he could and would take what he wanted.

So when a blanket fell over my body instead of Dutch's vile hands, I flinched, pulling against my bonds. But I didn't cry out. I kept my mouth shut and my fear firmly under control.

"I've got you, baby girl." Was that... was that my father?

"Daddy?"

"Yeah, baby. I'm getting you out of here."

"Atlas --"

"Don't worry. I'll take care of him." It didn't sound like Dad was particularly concerned about Atlas. In fact, he sounded like "taking care of him" meant he was going to hurt Atlas.

"Atlas!" I screamed for him. I needed to know where he was. If he was OK. "They had him tied up! Where is he?"

"Sting!" Dad looked over his shoulder, never slowing as he struggled to get the straps holding me to the stupid table loosened. "Get your man under control!"

"Atlas!" I sobbed out his name, my resolve finally slipping, knowing help had come.

An enraged roar answered my plea.

"Motherfuckin' leather straps," Dad muttered.

Finally, he got one of my arms free. Someone freed my head, and I raised up as far as I could. "Atlas!"

"You stay away from her, motherfucker!"

"Atlas, stop!"

"Get off me!"

I had no idea who surrounded me other than Alexei and Atlas, though I was pretty sure the one calling Atlas off was his president, Sting.

"Get him out of here before I fuckin' kill him, Sting. Now!" My dad snapped the order like he expected to be obeyed.

"Alexei, now's not the time."

"The hell it isn't! He kidnapped my daughter and took advantage of the situation he put her in!"

"Rose!"

There were sounds of a struggle, and I was pretty

sure everyone had forgotten about me. My hands were free, but my shoulders and ankles were still lashed down. I was helpless, and it was somehow worse than when I'd realized Dutch was going to brand me, because I couldn't see Atlas.

There was a fight. I heard grunts and angry yells combined with the sounds of flesh hitting flesh. The sounds weren't new, but they'd died down before. Now, it sounded like a whole new fight. Given everyone seemed to have forgotten about me, I figured it was Dad's Shadow Demons fighting the Iron Tzars.

I took a deep, calming breath, trying to get myself back under control. No one was going to release me until they were good and ready. Seemed like they were too busy fighting each other to worry about me.

Men.

Fuckers.

Somehow, I managed to wiggle under the strap holding down my upper back. The sweat coating my body eased the way slightly, but the fresh burn on my shoulder protested, the injured skin around the dead nerves nearly making me scream in pain. I held it in, just like I had earlier. Right now, the most important thing was getting to Atlas.

Once I'd wiggled under the strap, I was left with my ankles still lashed to the sides of the table. It took some doing, but I managed to push myself off the table to my feet, then sit down. I was naked as the day I was born in a room full of men. As I looked around, I saw several men lying on the floor, either dead or dying. All of them were Dutch's men. Dutch himself was slumped against the wall, where Atlas pounded the living fuck out of him.

There were four men -- one of them my dad -- trying to pull him off Dutch. Atlas just continued to pound the bastard. Blood was everywhere.

"Atlas! Help me! Please!" I sobbed out my plea, hoping to get him to look at me. To see my distress and come to me. When he didn't seem to hear me, I yelled louder. "Atlas! I need you! Now! Please! Please!"

This time, he turned his head to me, seeing me struggling to free my feet. Naked. On the floor.

Without a word, he shoved the men off him and stalked toward me. I was still fumbling with the strap on one leg when he freed the other and started on the one I was struggling with. The second it was off, I threw myself into his arms and burst into tears.

Atlas sat with me on the floor, one arm securely around me before he snagged the blanket that my father had draped over me and pulled it around me. "I've got you, baby. I've got you. Need to get you to a doctor."

"I've got one on standby." That was Azriel, my father's right hand and co-owner and co-founder of Argent Tech as well as the Shadow Demons. "We need to get her seen as quickly as possible so that burn doesn't get infected."

With those words, someone ripped me from Atlas's arms. I whimpered, reaching for him, but as Atlas stood, another man rested a hand on his shoulder and spoke quietly to him. I couldn't hear the conversation, but Atlas didn't follow. His gaze didn't leave mine, but he wasn't coming after me.

"Atlas?"

"I got you through this. Now, let your family take care of you. I'll be in touch."

"Like hell," my dad growled.

"Don't leave me, Atlas!" I was going to fall apart. I'd been with him for such a short time, but something inside me had bonded with him. I thought he'd felt the same way. Was I wrong? Hadn't he said he'd take care of me and any child I might be carrying? Had he changed his mind? That thought alone had me biting my lip to keep from continuing to beg him for his comfort.

"It'll all be fine, Rose. Everything will be fine." Atlas nodded at me, never taking his focus from mine.

As my father carried me out of the clubhouse and Atlas didn't follow, a sob of despair left me as everything I'd been through in the last few days finally hit home. I also realized that Atlas was wrong. Everything wouldn't be fine. Not even close.

Chapter Six
Bellarose

It had been two months since I'd last seen Atlas in that stupid compound. I'd kept to myself, mostly, only welcoming anyone in my suite of rooms for the therapy sessions Alexei and my mom insisted on. I'd also had a visit from a medical doctor who'd wanted to examine me the same day they brought me home. I'd refused to let him touch me other than to see to the brand burn. He'd given me a morning-after pill but, though I'd taken it from him, I'd flushed it after he left.

I had no right to hold on to Atlas like I was. He'd taken me in and protected me out of necessity. I'd explained to Dad how I'd come to be there, and he got it, but still couldn't see past what he saw as Atlas taking advantage of me. And yeah. He'd known we had sex. It was why he had me seeing the shrink. The same woman I was now sitting with, not saying a word.

The silence in the room was broken only by the ticking of a small clock over the fireplace mantel. I didn't feel like talking to the woman.

Finally, she spoke. "You don't seem to be making much progress past this," she said. Her name was Dr. Elizabeth Bailey. She looked to be in her mid-sixties and was very gentle in our sessions. I didn't want to like her, but I couldn't help myself. She'd been kind and caring, gently steering me in the direction she'd wanted me to go these last weeks. In all that time, she'd never mentioned my progress -- or lack thereof -- to me directly. She assured me she didn't tell my mother or father anything, though I had my doubts.

"What would constitute progress?" My question was quiet, and I didn't look at her -- rather I stared out the window at the world beyond the Shadow Demons' mansion.

"I don't know. It's relative, I guess. Have you left this house since being taken prisoner?"

"No. And I might have not been able to leave that place, but Atlas didn't take me as a prisoner. He took me to protect me. If he hadn't, I don't think the outcome would have been this good."

"So you don't blame Atlas?"

My gaze snapped to hers. "No. Not at all. He did everything he could to protect me."

"And the... intimacy?"

I sighed. "It was complicated. But not one-sided." I lowered my gaze before looking out the window again.

"I see. Have you spoken to him?"

I snorted. "You know I haven't. My dad won't hear of it, and I have no way of contacting him on my own. I didn't exactly get a phone number."

"All right. Tell me something, Bella. If you'd met Atlas under different circumstances, would you have looked twice at him?"

That surprised me enough to bring my full attention back to the doctor. "You mean, like if I'd met him at the school or in some other normal way?"

"Yes."

"I absolutely would have. When I first met him, he stopped to help me change a tire." I smiled at the memory. "He was charming and funny, once I got past the gruff exterior. Yeah. I'd have been open to getting to know him better."

"He's quite a bit older than you. You have to be able to see why your father has... reservations."

I snorted. "Yeah. Reservations. There's a word." I sighed bitterly. "Look. No offense, Dr. Bailey, but I don't want to move past Atlas. I don't want to forget him. He gave me some of the most wonderful moments of my life. Sure, there were bad things that happened. I've got the brand on me to prove it. But none of those were his fault. He kept me safe and called in help the second he could. If there was a delay, it was my fault. I wanted him to complete the work he was doing. I insisted. I still don't know if they caught the Swede. Or what eventually happened to Dutch."

Dr. Bailey smiled at me. "I'll tell your father you'd like to know. I'm also going to recommend he let the two of you meet. Whether or not he likes it, I believe it will go a long way toward you seeing reality for what it truly is. Might be good for your father too." Her smile was warm, but, I thought, calculating. Like she thought neither me nor my father would get what we thought out of that meeting.

After Dr. Bailey left, I went back to my window seat. It faced East. The direction I knew the Iron Tzars compound was. I had another reason for wanting to see Atlas. One I hadn't told anyone. A reason that morning-after pill was meant to take care of. I'd secretly hoped he'd been right and I'd conceived his child but hadn't really thought it was possible. Then the test I'd secretly ordered had presented me with two little pink lines.

I absently rubbed my lower belly and smiled to myself. Even if Mom and Dad didn't want me to see him, soon they wouldn't have much choice.

There was a knock at my door.

"Come in," I called softly.

"Bella?" My mother entered, immediately followed by Smokey the Second and Snowball the Third. The cats, who always seemed to know what I needed -- like their predecessors had when they'd first claimed me when I was six -- had found their way out of my room and to my mother.

"Hi, Mom."

"The cats pestered me until I came." She gave me a tentative smile. "I know you wanted to be alone, but I can't stand to see you hurting like this, sweetheart." She sat across from me on the window seat. "It breaks my heart."

It took everything inside me to not break down and cry. It was going to happen, but I was going to fight it as long as possible. Besides, my tears belonged to Atlas and no one else. Just like the rest of me.

"I can't feel anything other than what I do, Mom. I need to talk to Atlas."

"You only latched on to him because he was your lifeline, baby." She reached out and brushed a lock of hair off my cheek and tucked it behind my ear. "If you get out and do normal things, go back to the school to your job if you want, you'll be able to focus on something else. Then you'll see it was the forced proximity that made you feel the way you do. The school has been asking about you. They're anxious to get you back."

I turned back to look out the window again wistfully. "They just want to know if they need to replace me for the whole semester."

"Your father misses talking to you at breakfast and supper."

"I miss him, too."

"Come down and eat with us tonight. Ruth's having the kitchen make your favorite."

I smiled. Ruth had been having them make all my favorite meals and desserts since I came home, trying to get me to eat more. Trying to bring me as much comfort as she could.

"Meatloaf and mashed potatoes?"

"Think she's throwing in some mac and cheese too. And your favorite rolls."

"She's always trying to take care of me. You all do. I appreciate it, but this is something I'm going to have to work out myself." I smiled, trying to take the sting out of my words. "But I'll respect Ruth's and the staff's hard work and come to supper tonight."

"Thank you, sweetheart. I'll let your father know. I think Azriel and Giovanni would even come dine with us if they know you're coming."

"I'll be there."

* * *

Atlas

"Ain't ever been so uncomfortable in my Goddamned life." Who the fuck wore a monkey suit to dinner?

"Quit whining, Atlas." Alexei adjusted his cuffs and straightened his immaculate jacket. "If you want to see my daughter, you have to be able to function in her circles." The snotty bastard looked all superior and smug. Had he'd been the pussy businessman badass wannabe he presented to the rest of the world, I'd have punched the motherfucker. But Alexei and his associates were as highly trained as any member of Iron Tzars.

I still wanted to punch him, but I couldn't punish him for thinking I wasn't good enough for his daughter when I knew for a fact he was right. "Ain't whinin'. I know she's way outta my league. Why are you trying to make me look like the worst possible person for her?"

Giovanni snorted. "Because you were the experienced one in that encounter. You took advantage of a woman under your complete control, damn the consequences." I couldn't argue. I'd been beating myself up over that very same thing since the last time I'd seen her leaving with her family. "She might not have been able to reconcile her feelings with the reality of the situation, but you could. You saw a woman you wanted, and you took her."

"I know I'm a bastard, Alexei. I was a bastard to put her in that situation for any reason. I'll even admit that I thought I could keep her safe but that my job was more important than one woman. But it didn't take long for me to realize how fuckin' wrong I was. As to what happened between me and Rose --"

"Bella!" Alexei snapped, lunging for me and grabbing my throat. He shoved me against the wall and got right in my face, teeth flashing. "Her name is Bella! Or Bellarose. You will address her as such!"

I let Alexei do what he needed. It wasn't anything I wouldn't have done in his place.

"Come on, Alex. Let it go for now."

"This bastard…"

"We know what he did. We also know Bella's old enough to make her own decisions. As she told us, if she hadn't wanted to do something with him, she'd have gone down fighting."

Alexei bared his teeth at me again and shoved. Straightening his jacket once more, he turned his back on me and strode into the formal dining room.

The women were at the table. Alexei's wife, Rose's mother, Merrily, sat at the table with Rose. The two chatted lightly, if a bit more reserved than I'd have thought, and they didn't seem to notice the group of men approaching them. Alexei cleared his throat, and the two women faced us. Merrily smiled warmly, Rose gasped sharply. Her gaze zeroed in on mine, and she looked me up and down. When she looked at me once more, there were tears in her eyes she seemed to be trying desperately to hold back. She swallowed and hung her head, taking breath after deep breath. When she faced me again, her face was carefully blank.

"Welcome, Atlas," Merrily greeted. "Please sit down next to Bella."

Rose glanced up nervously before putting her head down once more. Was she ashamed to see me? Did I misread the whole situation? Maybe Alexei had been right. She'd realize how incompatible we were and tell me to fuck off.

"Hi." Rose breathed the word softly. Where she'd been so easy to read when I'd had her, now I had no idea what she was feeling.

"Hi, Rose," I murmured, leaning in to brush her cheek with a soft kiss. "You good?"

Alexei snorted behind me. "'You good.' Very smooth there, Atlas. Can't you string more than two words together?"

Rose trembled beside me, but she said nothing. She'd gone pale. It made my stomach turn to think she was so afraid of me. I knelt down beside her slowly so I didn't startle her. I moved my fingers to her jaw and brushed the skin lightly. "Look at me, honey. Please?" As she turned her head to obey me, two tears tumbled down her cheeks. "Are you scared of me? Are you afraid I'd hurt you?"

She shook her head, reaching out to my suit jacket. She patted my chest a couple times, like she was testing a hot surface. When she finally settled her hand still against me, her breathing came in pants, and she took great gulps of air. Then she dissolved into tears.

"Atlas!" She gasped my name as she threw herself into my arms, clinging to me as if her life depended on it. "I'm so sorry! I'm sorry!"

"Honey, what in the world? I'm the one who owes you an apology. You did nothing wrong."

"It wasn't your fault. And I don't regret it! I just... I don't want..."

"Honey, if you aren't comfortable with me being around you, I get it. I'm sure you'd rather forget we ever met, and I don't blame you."

"You... you wish we'd never met?"

I winced. Not at all. Obviously, she did. Should I be honest with her or say something to push her away? I knew what Alexei wanted me to do, but I couldn't bring myself to tell her I wished I hadn't met her. Because it'd be a Goddamn lie.

"You really *do* wish we'd never met." Her voice was flat and somehow disconnected.

"Not at all, baby. You're the best thing that's ever happened to me. I just hate it had to happen the way it did. You deserve better all the way around." I trailed my finger along her jaw. "You'll always mean the world to me. You can always come to me with anything. I'll always be there for you."

"You don't want me to stay with you. What we talked about..."

"Honey, I meant every word. But this is your choice. I think you know I'm not the kind of man to lie to you. Not when I put you under my protection. So when I told you I'd always be with you, I meant it. However you'll have me."

"Sit down, Atlas." Alexei, the bastard, wasn't ready to let me off the hook. "It's been hard on her since she got home safely. You're making it worse." When I shot him a look, he shrugged before continuing. "If you were the right man for her, you'd have kept any unpleasant conversation to yourself until after dinner. Like a civilized person. You'd have no idea how to function in her world. She deserves better. Someone who won't be an embarrassment to her."

"Daddy, Atlas could never be an embarrassment to me." She spoke softly. Almost as if she were afraid of Alexei when I knew she wasn't.

"He's a roughneck, Bella. Not even an officer in the armed forces. He's one of the lowest ranks there is because he has no education."

"That doesn't make him stupid, Dad. He figured out how to keep me alive. He listened to me and respected my evaluation of the situation and used it to his advantage when he could." Again, her voice was soft and subservient. This didn't seem at all like my Rose. My Rose followed my orders, but she had fire. Strength. Fierceness. She was a warrior as strong as any I'd ever known. This woman seemed too afraid of disappointing her father to make a strong case.

"Of course not, dear. But it means he'll never fit in with your social circle."

That seemed to take Rose aback. "Social circle?" She shook her head. "What social circle? I don't *have* a social circle! I've been in school and in training, trying to make you proud --" Her voice broke, and Alexei looked shocked, as if he had been expecting anything but the reaction he got.

"Alexei. Back off." Merrily put a hand on her husband's shoulder as she looked at me. "Bella feels a…" she glanced at her daughter briefly, "…certain connection with you, Atlas. She's young and hasn't been out in the world much. We've always been so protective of her, I guess we pushed her away. We don't expect you to feel the same connection she does. I don't think she expects it either. She just wants you to know she's wanted to talk with you since it happened."

"No one said I didn't feel the same way, Mrs. Petrov. I talked to a friend. She asked me if I'd have pursued Rose if we'd met under different circumstances. The only answer I had for her was yes. Absolutely. Had I known she was your daughter, I'd have gone about it a different way. Getting an audience with you through Sting or El Diablo. But I'd still have wanted to see her again."

"Why didn't you call in your team the second you realized who she was? Hell!" Alexei scrubbed a hand over his face. "You should have called a halt when you realized you had an innocent player in the crossfire. No matter who she fuckin' was!"

"He tried, Daddy." Rose looked up at her father, a small flash of something of the woman I'd grown to know over a few short days. "I insisted I'd do whatever he told me to. Follow his rules if he didn't call off his mission. I didn't want my life to be more important than the lives of so many others. Especially when there was a good possibility we could pull it off without putting me in unacceptable danger."

"That wasn't your decision to make, Bella. He knew that."

Rose opened her mouth like she might argue, then glanced at me, and her shoulders slumped. Whatever she'd been going to say died on her lips.

"Alexei," I stood, glaring at the other man. "I'd like a moment alone with your daughter. Please." Adding on the please made me want to puke, but I did it willingly. I needed to talk to Rose. To figure out what was going on inside her pretty head.

"Like hell," Alexei snapped.

"Alexei, stop." Merrily's voice rang out clear but

sounded more chastising than angry. "They went through a lot together. If Bella is willing to be alone with him, it's up to her."

Alexei looked at his wife like she'd grown two heads. "You can't possibly be serious."

"I am. Now, Bella? Do you want us to give you some privacy for a bit while you sort things out? If you don't, we won't abandon you."

"I know, Mom. Yes. I'd like to be alone with Atlas for a bit." She looked up at her dad. "And I mean alone, Dad. You make Giovanni put his bugs away. This is private."

"Baby..." He scrubbed a hand over his face wearily. "Fine. Thirty minutes." He glared at me. "Not a second more."

"Alex..." Merrily sighed. "As long as she needs, Atlas. But we'll check on you in ten minutes. If she wants to leave, I'm taking her out. If not, you'll have until she calls a stop to it."

I raised my chin in thanks to Merrily. Alexei scowled at me. "I didn't agree to this."

"No. You didn't." Merrily tugged him out of the room. "As her mother, I'm making an executive decision on this. She's not all right, and he's the only person who can help her understand their relationship."

Alexei pointed his finger at me. "You only get one shot. After that, I make you disappear."

"Understood. Sir." And yeah. "Sir" was harder than "please."

* * *

Bellarose

I'd only thought I'd been scared before. Sitting there with Atlas kneeling in front of me in my parents' formal dining room was even worse. This was a man who could shatter me so easily. I wanted to tell him how much I'd missed him. How I needed him in so many ways. But I didn't want to look like some girl with a teenage crush. It was so much more than that. At least, it was to me.

When the door to the dining room closed, Atlas pulled me to him, sitting me on his lap when he settled on the floor. The dam holding back my tears finally burst. I sobbed like my heart was breaking. And maybe it was. I'd experienced the most terrifying time of my life. At the same time, I'd experienced the most profound and beautiful pleasure I'd ever conceived of. How could I hate one and love the other when the terror made the pleasure possible?

"I'm sorry, Atlas. I'm sorry."

"You've got nothing to be sorry about. I'm sorry I didn't make more of an effort to talk to you. But you're dad's right. I'm not nearly good enough for you."

"You're everything I've ever wanted, Atlas!" I was still crying. Couldn't seem to stop crying. "I can't not have you in my life, but I can't see you with another woman either." I clung to Atlas, burying my face in his neck and inhaling deeply. I needed to take him into my soul so I could always have him.

"Honey, you never have to worry about seeing me with another woman. You're all I want or need. Remember I told you we'd table the relationship discussion?" When I nodded, he smiled gently at me. "Well, it's time to have it. Now tell me the truth. Do you want to see if we're right for each other? Because I think you're perfect for me."

My tears, which had started to slow, overflowed once more. "Me too. I want you, Atlas."

"You're dad's right about one thing. I'll never be able to give you everything he can. I'll never be able to give you everything you deserve. But I swear, I'll love you and adore you for the rest of my life."

"You can't know that you'll always love me. What if you grow to hate me?"

"Then you remind me why I love you. You smack me in the head. Or, better yet, go get your daddy. He'll beat some sense into me."

I couldn't help the small laugh that burst from me. "Are you sure this is what you want? To try to make a life together?"

"It is, baby. I think I knew way before the first time I kissed you. I think you had me with how fierce you looked holding that tire iron."

"There's something else." My heart was pounding now. I was really about to tell Atlas my secret.

"Tell me, baby."

I took a breath. "Remember when you asked me if I was on birth control?"

He grinned immediately. "I do. You sayin' I got one more claim on you? 'Cause, now that I know you're carryin' my kid, I'll have to keep you close. Ain't lettin' you outta my sight, woman."

"Do you promise, Atlas? Really promise?"

"Yeah, baby. I do. I swear I'll always keep you close."

When my mother knocked softly on the door and entered, Atlas still sat on the floor, holding me in his arms. He rocked back and forth, trying to soothe me.

"Atlas? Is she all right?" Merrily stood by the door, giving us privacy but keeping in clear sight of her daughter.

"She is. We both are. I need to talk with you and

Alexei, ma'am. It concerns the two of us."

"You're delusional if you think there's a 'two of us.' Bella is nothing to you." Alexei pushed his way past his wife and into the room.

"Afraid you're wrong, Alexei. I know you hate me and, like I said before, if I were in your position, I'd hate me too. But I will cherish her and protect her with everything in me for the rest of my life if you'll give your consent for us to give this a go."

"Absolutely not!"

"Alexei. Stop being an overprotective idiot." Merrily made the statement with a flippant wave of her hand, like she'd just dismissed her husband's objections because they were silly. I winced. This wasn't going to go well. For me. Everyone with a brain knew Alexei would never tell his wife she was being silly, so if he argued with her, he'd hurt her feelings. Which meant he was in a no-win situation, which gave him one more reason to hate me. "Bella is an adult. She can make her own decisions."

"She's not ready for a man like him, Merrily. He's a good man at heart, but he'll chew her up and spit her out!"

Merrily grinned. "I'm pretty sure I had that exact same thought about you when we first met, dear." Alexei shot her a look but didn't respond. Wise man.

"It's up to me to adapt if he tries to chew me up," Rose said, still clinging to me. "If he has to be what I need, I have to be what he needs, too. I promise, Dad. We'll work it out."

Alexei looked from his daughter to me and back several times. When he brought his focus back to me, his features hardened. "Again, Atlas. You're nothing to her. She's nothing to you. You were forced together under extreme circumstances. It created a false sense of intimacy --"

"Alexei, she's everything to me. She's also the mother of my child. That makes her mine. But it also makes me hers."

"What?" He barked out the question. "What do you mean she's the mother of your child? Are you fuckin' kiddin' me?"

"Afraid not. I didn't mean for it to happen, but I don't regret it. Only the circumstances around it."

Alexei was silent for a long time, just staring at me. Sizing me up one more time. "Just because you knocked my daughter up doesn't mean you get a hand in my money. You don't. I'll take care of Bella and her child, but you don't get one red cent."

"All right, that's enough," Merrily snapped. "Too far, Alexei." Her husband ignored her and continued.

"She's got your brand on her, you know." Dad's gaze narrowed. "Burned into her skin."

"I know where you're going with this, Alexei. It's already arranged. The second we get back to the Iron Tzars compound, it will be done. As to your money? I have no desire to take from you. I'll give Rose everything I can on my own. I may not be able to give her all the material things you can, but I'll give her all of me. My love and protection. Her and however many children she wants to give me. You can't buy love."

"You'd better. As to the other, I expect visual proof. I also expect you to give her everything she gave you."

"You can count on it, sir."

"Are you done, Alexei?" Mom didn't look happy. In fact, she looked like she wanted to stab her husband with a dinner fork.

"You knew this had to be done, Merrily."

"Atlas just told you you're going to be a

grandfather, and you're acting like you're ready to kill him." Mom looked like she was just shy of stomping her foot like an angry toddler. "Think about what he said and the impact it's about to have on your life, Alexei." She raised an eyebrow. "Grandpa. I think I like that better." She smirked before turning back to us. "Come now. Let's eat. You have a little one to feed and, if that child is anything like you were, you're about to have days you only wish you could eat." Mom smiled and reached out a hand for me. I went eagerly. Atlas stood and helped me into my chair before taking his own seat.

"Truce?" Atlas raised an eyebrow at Dad.

The other man snorted. "For now." Then he grinned. "Welcome to the family. Son."

Atlas groaned. "That one's gonna get old real fast."

Chapter Seven
Atlas

Dinner could have been the biggest disaster in the history of the world. Instead, it ended up being a very pleasant evening. Once Alexei made up his mind to embrace his daughter's wishes, he did so with gusto. Probably helped that we both respected each other. I knew he'd always have an eye on me, though. One misstep, and the man and his brothers knew how to make me disappear. Which didn't bother me, because I intended to make Rose so happy she never had reason to regret giving me a chance.

We'd ended the night in her bedroom. We made love, but mostly talked until the early morning. She'd missed me as much as I'd missed her, to my tremendous relief. It felt strange making love to my woman in her bedroom. I mean, the house was so enormous I could almost imagine it was a luxury hotel. But the fact was, I was fucking my woman in her parents' house. And I was a forty-one-year-old man, for crying out loud! Rose had gotten a kick out of that.

I'd taken her to my place in the Iron Tzars compound the next day. Now, we lay in *my* bed, naked and wrapped around each other. Rose dozed, but I fought sleep. I wanted to enjoy holding her for as long as I could.

"Atlas?"

"Yeah, baby."

"What happened to the Swede? Did you catch him?"

"We didn't. But your dad and his team did. As to what happened to him? I don't know. Though I have a good idea. Whatever they did, you can rest assured that guy will never harm another soul. Ever."

"What about Dutch?"

I was silent for a moment, looking down at her intently. "Don't ask unless you want to know, Rose. I won't lie to you, but that means you'll have to face some uncomfortable facts sometimes."

"Like what?"

"Like the fact that your dad and I both have something in common with each other. We're both killers. You may never see that side of either of us. But it's there. If ever there was a man who deserved those monsters, it was Dutch. And that whole stinkin' club."

"I understand. And yes. I still want to know."

"I beat him to death." I knew he told me the truth. I'd seen some of it. I think I knew in my heart that, when I called Atlas to me, it was already too late to prevent him from killing Dutch. It wasn't that I didn't want Dutch dead. The bastard needed to be sent straight back to hell where he came from. I just hadn't wanted it to be Atlas, because I didn't want that stain on his soul.

"I figured as much. If you're expecting me to be shocked and faint or some other hokey bullshit, don't hold your breath. That bastard deserved worse."

"He got worse. And he died. After a while."

"Good. I hate it had to be you who did it, but I can't be sorry you did. He hurt a lot of people."

"The only person I cared about him hurting was you, Rose. He was a dead man the second he touched you."

"Good. Then he wasn't shocked."

He grinned at me. "I didn't say that. I don't think he fully appreciated my abilities. He learned to, for all the good it did him. We also found several dozen more women and young girls. It's by no means everything, but maybe it stopped the trafficking in the immediate area."

"So everything you did, all the time you spent with those horrible people paid off."

"Hum... I don't know. I mean, I'd have given up on everything to keep you safe. I'm just sorry it took me so long to figure it out."

"I had to talk you out of calling in your team not two hours after you brought me back. I don't think that's a very long time."

"It was. Because I was honest with you before. You had me with the tire iron. I knew that very instant you were mine. I'd say the timing was piss-poor but maybe it was perfectly timed. If you'd been five minutes later, Dutch and his men would have found you instead of me. Then where would we have been? I should have called in my team the second I had the chance. I think that's the biggest reason your dad will have a hard time forgiving me or trusting me with your safety. I shouldn't have let you talk me into waiting."

"Well, it's done with now. I'm with you."

"Yeah. And you're with me."

* * *

Bellarose

He rolled us so that I lay beneath his much bigger body and settled himself between my thighs. His lips found mine, and he kissed me gently. Atlas had taken all kinds of time learning my body. Kissing every inch of skin he could get his lips on. He'd spent hours learning my body's responses. What brought me up slowly and what drove me mad. I had fun exploring him too. And Atlas had a magnificently wonderful body.

When he had me gasping in his arms, Atlas

entered me, pushing through my wet folds to fill me.

"Mmmm," I hummed my pleasure as he continued to kiss me. Would I ever get enough of this man?

"Mmmm," he hummed back, a slight chuckle in his voice. Then Atlas started to move inside me. Slow, deliberate strokes turned harder and more frantic. Finally, he surged forward into me. Deeper. Harder. Faster. When he slammed into me over and over, we both cried out, our bodies coated in sweat. My heart beat heavily, my exertion liberating.

"You're amazing, Rose. God, I love you!"

I shuddered against him. The words filled me with pleasure almost as great as the orgasms he'd given me. "I love you too, Atlas."

Once he'd cleaned me up, he lifted me from the bed and carried me to the closet. "Let's get dressed. There's something I have to do this morning, and I want you to be there before it starts."

"Well, that's not cryptic or anything."

He smiled at me. "It's nothing bad. Just something I need to do."

I tilted my head at him, thinking about something my dad had said. "Does this have anything to do with what you told my dad you'd set up for when we'd gotten back to the compound?"

"It is. You don't have to be there for the whole thing, but I'd like to start out the adventure with you at my side."

"You know I'll do anything you ask. If you want me there, I'll be there."

"Wait until you see what I'm doing. Then decide if it's something you can do."

"If it has to do with you, I can." I stuck out my chin. "I will."

"I love how fierce you are!" He leaned in to take my mouth again. "Makes me want to fuck your sweet mouth to get you to shut up."

I swat at him playfully. "You're horrible."

"I know. But I think that's part of why you love me."

It totally was.

Once we were dressed, Atlas took me to a barn off in the field behind the main clubhouse. Inside were several members of his club. Everyone was silent and stood around a table that looked suspiciously like the one Dutch had bound me to. I shivered in reaction, my gaze finding Atlas's.

"I'm branding myself with *your* property patch. I'm yours. You're mine."

"No." I shook my head fiercely, terrified for him as I remembered how badly it hurt me. "Atlas, you don't have to do this." The thought of him going through the same thing I had, to feel his skin sizzling and smell his own flesh burning… I didn't want that for him. Not for any reason. "You can get a tattoo or something. I don't care. But I don't want you doing this."

"I'm doing it, baby. And I'll endure it as well as you did. Not a sound."

"But, Atlas…"

"Not. A. Sound. You did it for me. I'll do this for you."

"If you're doing this because my dad's an asshole, don't. You don't have to prove anything to him."

"I'm not trying to prove anything to him. Or even to you. I'm doing this for me. Because you endured something that horrible in silence. Because I told you to."

"It was to keep us both safe. I know why you did it."

"Maybe. More, though. I wanted to give you something to concentrate on so you would get through it. If you were concentrating on trying not to scream, I knew your stubborn nature would kick in, and you'd keep silent as a way to tell that fuckin' bastard to go to fuck himself."

"You wouldn't be wrong."

"Of course, I'm not. Now. Come with me. Once everything's ready, you can leave."

"No. I'm staying. I'll hold your gaze through the whole thing like you did me. You grounded me. Helped me hold on to my sanity."

"My brave, fierce girl."

"Take off your shirt," Sting commanded. He stood next to the table. Brick sat on a bench on the other side of Sting, heating the branding iron with a torch.

Atlas whipped off his shirt before handing it to me and kissing my lips lightly. He moved to the table and let the men strap him down much the same way I'd been. I approached the table, my gaze locked on his.

"You sure you want to do this, Atlas?" Sting asked the question with a raised eyebrow, like he thought Atlas should change his mind but knew he wouldn't.

"I am." Atlas never broke eye contact with me. "I'll accept Rose's property patch the same as she accepted mine."

"Deep breath," Sting muttered. Then he touched the brand to Atlas's shoulder in the same place Dutch had placed my brand.

Atlas flinched once, but otherwise took the pain in silence. After several ragged breaths, he made an effort to slow his breathing, to take several deep breaths. Someone draped a cool towel over his back.

"Give us a second to undo the straps." Atlas nodded, not saying a word. I could see beads of sweat on his forehead and across his nose. I knew well the pain he'd just endured. I was glad his brothers were there to make the aftercare easier. I didn't want this for him, but since he'd done it, I was determined to never let him regret it.

Stitches, the club's doctor, had applied some ointment to the burn and given him two different creams for it to apply a couple hours apart. He also gave Atlas a pain shot.

"I'll come back to check on you guys in a few days. If you think it looks infected, or hurts more than it should, let me know immediately."

"I'll make sure he does." I looked up at Atlas, so proud I could burst. I hated the pain for him, but the fact he'd done it for me, because he wanted me to know I was important to him, made me want to cry with happiness. I was grabbing on to him with both hands and not ever letting go.

"You can make all the fuss over me you want, darlin'. I'll do my best to get all the sympathy you're willin' to dish out." He winked at me when I was sure he was in enough pain to not feel like being lighthearted. He was doing it for me.

For me!

After the burn was dressed, Atlas put his shirt back on. "I'll take you back to the house, then I have a meeting with Sting. Feel free to explore. Just don't leave the compound unless you tell someone. I have to know where you are so you don't try to slip away from me."

"No need to worry about that, but I promise I

won't leave without telling someone."

"You're an amazing woman, Bellarose. I'll spend my life worshiping you and loving you."

"I swear you'll never regret what you did today. I didn't like watching you go through it, but I figured if you could be there with me, I could do the same for you. Thank you for the gesture, too. It means a lot."

"You're worth everything, Rose. There's only one thing we need to get straight."

"Oh? What's that."

"This baby." He caressed my belly before lifting my shirt and placing a kiss just below my navel. "It better be a boy. I've seen what having girls does to men, and I'm not sure my man card would survive a daughter."

I laughed. "I'll do my best to honor that request. But I make no promises."

"As long as I have you, it doesn't matter. You and our child."

"I love you, Atlas. Thank you for everything. For fighting for me."

"I'm just sorry I didn't do it sooner."

"We're together now."

"Yeah, baby. And that's all that matters."

Warlock (Black Reign MC 9)
A Bones MC Romance
Marteeka Karland

Warlock: Love didn't stop me from killing my ex when I had to -- wasn't a choice I made lightly, but more lives than hers were on the line. Black Reign gave me the second chance I didn't deserve, and never again would I put a woman above my club.

Then along comes this little vagabond who claims my mother left me to her in her will. Is that even possible? And to top it off, it looks like my mother pulled some strings and got us married. Without my consent. Still, I think I'd rather be married to the crazy woman my mother foisted off on me than play Santa at the club's annual Christmas party. Yeah. *Not* a role I'm made for.

Hope: Christmas magic being what it is, maybe I can get my fondest wish this year. To say Warlock isn't happy when he finds out he's married to me is the biggest understatement in the history of understatements. Still doesn't make me want my fantasy lover any less.

Warlock represents everything I've ever wanted in life. But the fact that I achieved my dreams through more manipulation -- even if it wasn't of my doing -- means I have to give him up. But first, Warlock has to see beyond his past and embrace a future he never wanted.

Prologue
Warlock

"Shh, Bev. Look at me."

"I don't want to look at you, you bastard!"

"But you will. You shared my bed. I gave you everything you ever wanted. Gave you more than I was prepared to give when I met you but did it willingly. The least you can do is look at me now."

Bev finally looked up at me. I cupped her face gently, needing to look into her beautiful, deceitful eyes one last time. I wanted to remember the good times but struggled to recall any. She'd used me from the first day I'd met her and her daughter. She'd cost me everything. My club. My self-respect. My brothers. Even my son.

I bent to kiss her. Her lips were as sweet as ever, but there was more of a saccharine sweetness than there had ever been before. I lingered only a moment before I lifted my head. I retained my gentle hold on her face, knowing what I was about to do, but praying she didn't. I gazed down into her eyes before shifting my hold slightly and wrenching her head hard to the right, snapping her neck.

The second her neck broke, Bev's body collapsed. I caught her and sank to the ground, raising my face to the sky to bellow in pain. I'd loved her. So fucking much. She hadn't loved me back. She'd deceived me. Probably from the first day we'd met. But, to me, it had all been real.

Now I had nothing. My son, Sting, was now president of Iron Tzars, and I was gone. I'd always be there for him if he needed me, but I knew I was dead to him. With good reason. By knowingly allowing Bev to manipulate me, I'd betrayed the club. They should have killed me, but Sting had made an exception because of my years of service to the club. It was a weakness I prayed didn't come back to haunt him later. I'd caused enough trouble in his life without that.

I'd never have my family back. All because of this unworthy woman. I comforted myself with the fact that her daughter, Chloe, had found a good home and a strong protector. I wasn't sure what I'd do with my life now, but one thing was for damned sure. I was never getting involved with another woman.

Chapter One
Warlock
One Month Later

"You're out of your Goddamned mind, Samson."

"El Diablo says you're the one for the job. He's president. His word is law."

"No fuckin' way." I missed the day when that particular growl of displeasure sent men scurrying off to do my bidding. Those days were over now. I was barely more than a prospect with this new club. Black Reign was similar to Iron Tzars in that they pretty much did as they pleased. They tried to look all badass and shit, but they catered to their women worse than even Bones. Especially the girl children. The boys learned to protect the girls and took their roles seriously. While I appreciated the sentiment, my wound was still too raw.

"Well, you're free to leave. No one's stoppin' ya."

"What the fuck, Samson? I've done everything this club has asked of me since I got here! Surely to fuckin' God, there is someone else better qualified to do this!"

"Probably. El Diablo says he wants you." Samson looked me up and down, shaking his head in disapproval. "God only knows why."

"This is absurd. I ain't doing it."

"Stop being such a fuckin' pussy, Warlock. Everyone takes a turn. Even El Diablo, though he loves it. This year it's your turn. Low man on the totem pole."

"I didn't sign up for this."

"Nope. You got drafted. Get used to it. You got a couple weeks to come to terms with the fact that you're gonna be the Jolly Old Elf." Samson, the bastard, grinned like a motherfucker. "You'll be thankful when the kids get to the party. Besides, this is Dawn's favorite part of the Christmas party. You don't put on your best Santa Claus performance, El Diablo will have your balls."

"He wants his daughter to not be disappointed, he needs to get someone else. I ain't no fuckin' Santa Claus."

Samson shrugged as he turned to go. "You don't wanna do it? You tell El Diablo yourself. It's your funeral, pal."

Fuck. I didn't fuckin' need this.

I snagged the freshly dry-cleaned Santa suit from the bar where Samson had laid it. The prospect snickered but quickly turned his back. Normally, I'd have punched the motherfucker in the face, but it didn't seem worth the Goddamned trouble. Looked like I was stuck on Santa duty.

Fuck... fuck.

I stalked to the room I'd been given a month ago. The only things in the place were a few changes of clothes and a bed. I hung the fucking Santa suit on the bathroom door and sat on the bed, scrubbing a hand over my face.

When I'd come to this place, it was because Cain told me El Diablo had requested me. From what I'd gathered, it was more of an order than a request. I'd needed to get as far away from the Iron Tzars as I could, and Fort Worth, Florida had seemed to fit the bill. Besides, I was curious about El Diablo and what he wanted with me. He was a legend in the MC world. Not because he was so flamboyant, though he could be that on occasion, but because of his secretiveness. The only thing most people ever heard about were the raucous parties held at Black Reign or the help they gave the community. Like this fucking Christmas party coming up. But those of us deep in the MC world knew El Diablo was much, much more than what was on the surface.

I lay back on the bed with a groan. I was too fucking old for this shit. With perfect timing, my phone rang. I knew without looking it would be El Diablo.

"I need a word with you, Warlock." His clipped British accent always threw me off.

"Yeah? If it's about the Santa gig you can shove it up your ass."

His boisterous laughter set my teeth on edge. "Now, now. Everyone takes a turn."

"Yeah? Get someone who's been here longer than a fuckin' month to do it."

"Nope. It's all you, my friend. Now. Come to my office. We need to have a chat."

Fuck. I didn't need this. If I wasn't curious as hell, I'd get on my bike and… *ride*. Never come back. I'd disappear into the great beyond and never be seen or heard from again. But I *was* curious. A man like El Diablo didn't request you join his club to be fucking Santa Claus.

I made my way to the president's office. Club girls rubbed against me several times on the way. I was still the new fish, and they were all looking to land me. None of them were appealing in the least. Every time I looked at one of them, I saw Beverly. The woman I'd loved and had to kill. They were every bit as manipulative as Bev had been, but they didn't try to hide it. That was something at least. Didn't mean I'd ever give any of them the time of fucking day.

"What's on your mind, El Diablo?" I plopped down on the leather couch in his office. I hadn't bothered to knock, hoping to irritate the man a little bit. Of course, it didn't.

"Warlock." He grinned as he leaned back in his chair, steepling his fingers. "How are you settling in?"

"Was doin' fine."

"I imagine you'll feel much better about your situation after the Christmas party. It's actually an honor to be chosen Santa."

"I thought everyone took a turn?"

He waved me off. "That's the idea, but there are certain members who wouldn't be a good fit for the role."

I raised my eyebrows. "And you think I will be?"

"Oh, absolutely. You need to find your footing. Find that... inner peace you've been searching for."

For a moment, I couldn't find my voice. When I did, it came out harsher than I intended. "Are you out of your fuckin' mind? Do you have any idea what I've been through?"

Instantly, El Diablo's face hardened. "I do, indeed. And if it weren't for me, your own son would have probably waited for the right moment, then put a bullet in your Goddamned head."

I'd known this. Had anticipated it. But I'd been so far gone in my self-pity and self-loathing, it hadn't really sunk in that, as president, since I was his father, Sting would have taken the responsibility for exacting justice for the club himself. My choices had put the club squarely in the path of the CIA. If he didn't go after me, it would have made him look weak. For a newly appointed president of a powerful MC, that would have been a death sentence for him. We'd had our differences in the past, but we loved each other. I'd taught him no one was above club law. Not us. Not our families. I'd reinforced that notion when I'd killed Bev.

I'd left it up to him to exact club law on me.

I sighed. "Shoulda ended it all instead of coming here. That woulda saved everyone the fuckin' trouble."

"Now you really do sound like a pussy." El Diablo scowled, looking at me in disgust. He was right. I had a horrible case of feeling sorry for myself. "Take the second chance offered you. While I don't condone the way you handled yourself with Ms. Martin, the fact that you took responsibility for her yourself tells me what I need to know about your character. Your woman never loved you. Not the way you loved her. Your mistake was in staying with her when you knew that, not only did she not love you, but was using you to get inside your club."

"You think I don't know my mistakes?" I snapped. "I'm fully aware of everything I did. I'm also aware I looked like a fool for trying to hang onto a woman who didn't want me."

He shrugged. "The heart wants what it wants."

"If I'd grown a pair before when I realized what she was up to, she'd still be alive."

"Doubtful. If it hadn't been you, she'd have found someone else and likely had a more gruesome death. Most MCs tend to make examples of people who betray them."

"Why am I here, El Diablo?" I wanted this done so I could go back to my room and slash that fucking Santa costume to ribbons. Might make me feel better.

"I have a position for you in Black Reign."

I shrugged. "Not news. I'm here. I do whatever you ask me to do. I'm a glorified errand boy tasked with being Kris fucking Kringle. Other than that, I've never complained."

"Not exactly what I was talking about, but as long as you're aware you still have to play Santa, I'll call it a win. No. I want you to be Black Reign's Enforcer. You'll answer to Razor as Sergeant at Arms. You'll enforce our rules and carry out any punishments necessary."

"No." I shook my head. "Not happening. I'm done with being an officer in any club."

"You'll do what I tell you to, Warlock. This is where you're needed. It's what I'm demanding of you." Where before he looked relaxed, now El Diablo was hard and all business. This was the legend no one fucked with.

"I'll think about it." It was the best I could offer him. At least, until I could convince him I wasn't the man for this fucking job.

"You have until tomorrow. Your residence here is dependent on your decision."

"That all?" If the bastard thought that was going to sway my decision, he could fucking think again.

"Yes." He dismissed me with a wave of his hand. Looked like I was packing. Because there was no way in hell I was getting deep into the workings of Black Reign. Being an officer of any kind would demand I be involved. Well, at least leaving meant I wouldn't have to go to the fucking Christmas Party.

As I entered the common room, I heard a feminine voice. One I hadn't heard in the clubhouse before. It was sweet and pure, wrapping around my insides and squeezing painfully. I remembered that sensation and didn't welcome it. The difference was, this time, it was ten times stronger than it had been with Bev. I knew I needed to sprint as far away from that fucking voice as I could, but my eyes automatically scanned the room looking for the source. When I found her, I nearly fell to my knees, crawled over to her, and fucking *begged* her to be mine.

She looked to be about twenty (I hoped) with jet-black hair so curly it looked like she hadn't brushed it in several months. At the roots where her natural color had grown out, it was a bright, flaming red. Looked like she'd tried to cover it up but was in need of a touch-up job. Her skin was pale with freckles everywhere. Short and slight of stature, she might have weighed ninety pounds. Soaking wet. On her face was one of the most gloriously beautiful smiles I'd ever seen in my lifetime. Her skin was sprinkled liberally with freckles I wanted to trace with my tongue. She wore cut-off jeans shorts that came above her knees and looked like they were at least two sizes too big, and a stained AC/DC T-shirt. How a woman so disheveled and odd-looking could be so appealing to me at first glance was a total fucking mystery. I liked my life orderly. My women sure of themselves. This girl was anything but. Chaos embodied. That's what she was.

"I'm looking for Maximilian Wagner?" She spoke to the prospect at the bar who grinned at her. I frowned. If I hadn't already been focused on her, I was now. No one *ever* called me by that name. Well, except my mother, but we hadn't spoken in more than fifteen years. Her decision. Not mine.

"Not sure I know anyone here by that name, sweets." Then he tilted his head. "Are you even old enough to be in here? How'd you get through the gate?"

"Well, I told that guy --" She hiked a thumb over her shoulder in the general direction of the front gate. "-- Who I was looking for. He made a call, then let me in." She shrugged. "I assumed he got permission from someone because he was very adamant no one was to be here unless they were with a member or had special permission." She held out a piece of paper in her hand to the prospect. "I got special permission." The girl looked supremely satisfied. "And I'm twenty-two. Ish."

"Yeah? It's the 'ish' part that makes my eye twitch. Gimme some ID, sweets." He ignored the paper and held out his hand. I wanted to intervene, but there was no way I was getting into the discussion if this girl was looking for me. Who the hell would know to send her here and how the hell did she know my name? Because there was no way there were two Maximilian Wagners in this fucking compound.

With a sigh and after much digging through the hideously oversized bag she carried like a purse, she pulled her ID out and handed it over.

"Twenty-two, huh?"

"I said ish."

"You're nineteen."

"Almost twenty!" Her eyebrows narrowed, challenging the big biker, who was easily twice her size.

"You lack two months, sweets. And twenty is not twenty-one."

"Well, it's not like this is a public bar. I'm sure there are plenty of people here under twenty-one."

"Only a couple of the ol' ladies, and they never drink unless their men are with them. You got a man?"

"Well, yes. I do, actually." She handed the paper to him once more. "Maximilian Wagner. He's mine. So, yes. I have a man."

A couple of things went through my mind at that point. The first thought was, "Yes. Yes, I am." Immediately on the heels of that thought was, "Are you fuckin' kiddin' me? I never want another woman in my life as long as I fuckin' live!"

"Last Will and Testament?" The prospect studied the document intently for several seconds. "This woman -- Verna Wagner -- left her son, Maximilian Wagner, to you in her will? Like, for real?" He looked up, as bewildered as I was angry. "You know she can't do that. Right? You can't leave a person to someone in a will. That's insane."

"It's exactly something my mother would try to do." My voice was much harsher than it needed to be, but it seemed my mother hadn't changed a bit. Still trying to control my life. "I'm Maximilian Wagner. How do you know my mother?" It was nothing more than a demand. I did it deliberately, because I knew that particular tone made even the most seasoned bikers think twice about defying me. Or staying in the same room with me.

The girl's head snapped around the second I spoke, so she looked at me, her eyes wide. As she took in my appearance and countenance, her eyes got even wider, and she paled even more. The closer I got, the more alarmed she grew, and began to back away from me. It ended with her giving a cry as she stumbled backward until she tripped over a chair. She tumbled to the ground, crab-walking backward until she hit the wall.

"Well?" I held my hands out to my sides. "Here I am. Maximilian Wagner in the fucking flesh. What do you want?"

"I-I..." She swallowed, then lifted her chin. Seeming to realize she was on her ass on the floor of the clubhouse, she scrambled to her feet, still staying a good distance away from me. I noticed she wore canvas shoes with more than one hole in them and no socks. Girl looked like a street urchin. Then, with an amazing impression of my mother, she spoke. "Mrs.

Wagner told me I should find you and let you know your roaming days are over." She would have sounded more confident if her voice hadn't been wavering and her hand shaking as she pointed to the paper the prospect behind the bar held. She also sounded like she was saying something she'd rehearsed over and over. It was probably a script my mother had given her to memorize.

"My roaming days."

"Yes. I'm to make an honest man of you." That got a bark of laughter from the prospect before he turned away, clearing his throat to cover it.

"Honest man." I know I sounded like a parrot, but this was too much to take in.

"Well, yes. She said she was giving you to me. So. You're mine."

I shook my head, the whole thing surreal. Not making any sense. "All right. Let's start over. Who the fuck are you?"

She winced, either at my language or my furious expression. I didn't know which. Didn't much care. "My name is Hope." Immediately she started digging in her bag again. The thing was so big it could have carried an assault rifle and I wouldn't have been surprised.

"Hope… what?"

"Um, well…"

"Girl, I'm losing my patience."

"Until a week ago, it was Hamilton." She was still digging in her bag, and I was beginning to think she might be slightly crazy.

I knew better than to ask my next question, but I couldn't help myself. It slipped out before I could censor it. "What happened a week ago?"

She looked up and smiled brightly. "I got

married!"

"Um, OK…" But it wasn't OK. First, if she was married, where the fuck was her man? No man worth a good Goddamn let his woman walk into a biker compound by herself. Second, if she was married, it meant I couldn't have her. Which I was relieved about. Really! I was forty-nine years old. I had a twenty-eight-year-old son, for fuck's sake! What the everlasting fuck would I do with a nineteen-year-old crazy woman? "Where the fuck is your husband?"

Now, her smile faltered as she slowly handed me an envelope. It was official looking, and I had a feeling I was about to lose my ever-loving shit. I snatched it away from her, and she flinched. The envelope had originally been opened very carefully. As if whatever inside was important, and the recipient didn't want to damage the envelope or the contents. I yanked the paper inside out, tossing the envelope to the floor. It ripped in the process. Immediately, Hope dove for it, picking it up and smoothing it where I'd crumpled it and smoothing down the edges I'd ripped, confirming my suspicions. Whatever this was, it meant something to her.

I scanned the paper. Immediately I recognized it as a marriage certificate. I glanced up at her. She seemed to hold her breath, nibbling on her bottom lip. As I returned my focus to the paper, the door to Shotgun's office was jerked open and Esther, Shotgun's woman, ran out of the room and straight to Hope. The woman stood solidly in front of Hope, backing the other woman away from me as she spoke softly.

"Uh, Warlock?" I glanced to my right where Shotgun came out of his office. "Might, uh… Might wanna lay that down and go back upstairs."

Naturally, that wasn't happening. "Not now,

Shotgun." I scanned the document. Sure enough, there was my name in bold black letters. Right alongside Hope's. "Are you fuckin' kiddin' me?"

"Well, no. If you'd look at Mrs. Wagner's will, it will explain everything."

"My mother was as manipulative as my fuckin' ol' lady. Anything she did was with the sole purpose of makin' my life miserable."

"Come on, honey," Esther said, trying to coax the young woman into Shotgun's office. "Let's go talk about this somewhere more private."

Hope looked distressed, but resisted Esther's efforts to remove her from the situation. "But I want my marriage certificate back," she said. "And Mrs. Wagner's will. They're mine!"

"I know, honey. I know. I'll get them back for you, but let's go to the office."

"There's no way this is fuckin' real." I waved the certificate at Hope, crumpling it in my fist. Her gaze was glued to it, her lips parted in a gasp as if I'd destroyed her most prized possession.

"Please! Give it back! Give it back!"

"Did you make it or did my mother?"

"The state of Indiana made it! No one else!" She looked desperate. Near tears. When she broke away from Esther, she reached for the paper and pried it out of my hands. I was only too happy to let it go. Knowing what it was, holding it in my hand... It felt like a hot branding iron, imprinting this girl on my skin. Into my life. I actually rubbed my hand on my jeans, trying to shake that sensation. It had to be fake. But, somehow, I knew it wasn't.

"She's not lying, Warlock." Shotgun put himself between me and Hope, his hand on my shoulder. "I started looking her up the second she walked through the gate and we knew her name. As of eight days ago, she's Mrs. Maximilian Wagner."

"Well, obviously I didn't consent. *Fix this*!" As angry as I tried to look, there was a curious mix of titillation alongside the anger. "This is just like my mother. Always putting herself before anyone in her life."

"You take that back!" Hope let Esther have the certificate of marriage. Probably because the other woman was helping her straighten out the crumpled parchment. "Mrs. Wagner was the kindest, most thoughtful person I've ever met in my life!"

"Yeah? You shoulda had her for a parent," I snapped. "Woman never did anything but criticize me. Did you know she refused to speak to me after I joined Iron Tzars? She was a professor of law at Maurer School of Law. You think she wanted it known her son was in an MC? It didn't matter that anything shady we did was to help people. We were still vigilantes, and that went against everything she'd stood for her whole life."

"Well, could you blame her?" Hope stood nose to… well, nose to chest with me. She was a tiny thing, but she had bite. Like an angry Chihuahua. She might be small, but she could leave scars on a man's ankles. Which did nothing to cool the arousal I'd started feeling toward this girl. "Her whole life was dedicated to the law. She believed in the justice system with everything in her. She believed that, while things didn't always turn out the way we wanted or hoped, the justice system in America worked. Having a son who routinely took the law into his own hands wasn't something she could accept easily."

"Or at all. She tell you it's been more than a decade since we've spoken?"

"Yes. She said it was something she deeply regretted. We talked about it and, while she never fully accepted that you're a vigilante, she said she wished she'd figured out a way for the two of you to work together for the betterment of the people in your community. She said she'd since realized that you picked up where the law couldn't intervene."

"Well, bully for her. She finally got it." I knew I was belligerent, and Hope didn't seem like a girl who could take me in this kind of mood, but I couldn't seem to stop myself from pushing her. "I want to go back to the part where she left me to you in her will."

"I realize that sounds a bit unusual, but it was her wish that I find you and see to it you had a woman in your life to make you happy." She tried to give me a small smile that seemed a little too close to tears of anger, instead of like she was as happy about it as she'd been when she first entered the clubhouse.

"The very last thing in need in my life right now is another woman. Do you want to know what happened to my last ol' lady?"

"That'll do, Warlock." El Diablo's voice commanded obedience. He stood on the second-story landing above the common room, his woman, Jezebel, at his side. Both looked disapproving. Straight at me.

"There's no reason to be a complete bastard." Jezebel aimed an indignant sniff in my direction. "Besides, you have no idea what might have prompted this gesture on the part of your mother."

"And, of course, *you* do, Jezebel." I didn't make it a question, and it was more of a mocking tone than El Diablo would allow and I knew it.

"Watch your tone with my wife, Warlock. That's your only warning." The look in the president's eyes was the look of the man I expected to find the first time

I'd set foot into Black Reign's territory. He was a straight-up killer. Which was fine by me. I was too.

"I have no idea what would prompt a mother to give her son to someone in her will. But I imagine it was for the good of those she loved. Especially since she seems to have forced the issue by marrying the two of you," Jezebel continued as if neither I nor El Diablo had spoken.

Touché.

El Diablo and Jezebel came down the stairs and into the crowd that had formed around me and Hope. Jezebel left his side to go to Hope, taking her hands. "Do you know why Mrs. Wagner would do this, Hope?"

The girl looked down, her shoulders slumping. I got the impression she was trying like hell not to lose control, but this simple question was pushing her to her limit. "I do."

When she didn't offer anything else, Jezebel prompted gently. "And?"

"She wanted me to have something of my own. Mrs. Wagner didn't have anything to give me other than her son. So, she gave him to me."

"Why not give you a puppy dog. Or a fuckin' cat?" Yeah, I was an asshole, but my mother and her highhandedness always put me in a bad fucking mood.

"Because she didn't have anything. Or anyone." Hope looked up at me, anger and grief on her lovely face. "No one but me."

"Why not leave you the house or her bank account or any number of things? What the fuck are you playing at?"

"She had nothing!" Hope's voice wavered, but I got the feeling this was still as much anger as it was because she was sad or grieving and struggling not to cry. "She was sick. Couldn't take care of herself. When she got sick, she ended up in the hospital. Once she was better, she couldn't go home because she was too weak to walk. So she went to a nursing home. Medicare only pays for about a hundred days of skilled nursing care. Once that ran out, she had to pay for it on her own." Hope dashed away a tear that had overflowed and run down her cheek. "She was there for five years before I met her. I volunteered after school and met her there. She said that she'd always intended to die in her home, so hadn't bothered to get other health insurance. It cost her everything."

"I find it hard to believe my mother would go to all this trouble to repay you for a friendship you forged while she was in a nursing home. You spent, what? A couple hours through the week with her?"

"I was there every afternoon after school until visitation hours were over and all day on the weekends! She had me read my homework to her, and she helped me with it. Her body was weak, but she had as sharp a mind as I've ever known. She was so smart and wanted to see me do well in school. I wanted to have something to offer when I met the right man. She said a keen mind and a kind heart were the best things anyone had to offer a prospective mate."

"Still not buying it." I was missing something. Or, rather, Hope was keeping something from me.

"I guess it doesn't matter," she said, pulling away from Jezebel and taking the marriage certificate and my mother's will. Carefully, she refolded them, tucked the marriage certificate back in the now-ripped envelope, then put both of them in her bag. "I'm sorry to have disrupted your day." Her tone was polite, but her chin trembled and tears glistened in her eyes. I felt like I'd kicked a puppy.

She turned to go when Esther reached out to her, gently turning Hope to face her. "You're leaving out part of your story, Hope. Did your upbringing have anything to do with Mrs. Wagner's gesture?"

Hope shrugged. "Yes. Those reasons are my own, though. I promised Mrs. Wagner I'd find her son and try to convince him to make this work. I can see now this was one more fantasy to add to a long list of them."

"I don't fuckin' need this," I muttered, scrubbing a hand over my face. "Tell me, Hope. What is it that made my mother think she could give me to you?"

Chapter Two
Hope

I grew up in a world where everyone looked down on me, but never in my life had I met someone who disliked me so intensely in so short a time. Every word out of Maximilian "Warlock" Wagner's mouth was one more knife in my heart. He was destroying my dream and didn't even care. I knew Mrs. Wagner's promises were far-fetched and more the musings of an old, regretful woman than anything truly attainable, but she'd convinced me everything would work out. This man hadn't cared about his mother's wishes or even the feelings of a woman standing in front of him. Sure, I was naive to have believed Mrs. Wagner's plan would work, but this man was beyond cruel.

He was also the most gorgeous man I'd ever seen. Tall, thickly built with an abundance of muscle, Warlock had the look of a dangerous man. One who could hurt anyone he took a disliking to if he chose. His hair and beard were mostly white, and there were fine lines around his eyes and his brow, but that was the only indication of his age. Mrs. Wagers said he was forty-nine. The age gap had seemed daunting then. Now, I knew I was in over my head even as I desperately wanted him to claim me as I'd tried to claim him.

I thought about his question. What would make his mother think she could give him to me? "She'd hoped I could bring something to your life. That I could help you make a home and have a happy life."

"What makes you think I'm not happy with my life, huh? I had an ol' lady. We weren't legally married, but in my world we might as well have been."

That took me by surprise. "I-I'm sorry," I said.

"I'm sure Mrs. Wagner had no idea."

"Because she refused to talk to me. She knew how to get a hold of me if she wanted to talk. I know because I made sure she did. If she was so concerned about me, she should have called." He stopped his tirade abruptly, tilting his head as if something occurred to him. "She would have looked into whether or not I was married before she did this. This thing, this whole scheme wasn't about me. This was about you."

I bit my lip, not liking his insight. I didn't want to talk about this anymore. It was uncomfortable and, honestly, why had I expected this would end any other way?

With a shrug, I slung my bag over my shoulder. "It doesn't matter. This was more than anyone could be expected to handle civilly." I wanted out of here. "This was a huge mistake, and I apologize to have taken it so far."

"That's all well and good, but we're married. This has to be dealt with." Maximilian -- Warlock -- didn't look as furious and frustrated as he had moments ago. I wasn't fooled, though. This man wanted me gone, but he likely wanted the complication I represented gone even more. Which was our marriage, questionable as it was. It tore my heart out to think about giving up that tie I had to someone. The only tie to another person I'd ever had in my life.

"I can get it annulled on the grounds of fraud, since you didn't know about it and couldn't legally consent to it." The one he'd called Shotgun shrugged, bracing his hands on the back of a nearby couch. "Will take time. Also, it might open her up to legal action from the state. I'll have to check with Wrath."

"You can't do that, Warlock." Big and scary as he was, Jezebel wasn't intimidated by Warlock at all. Of course, her husband was even more intimidating than Warlock, so that shouldn't have surprised me. "Figure something else out."

"Not my problem, Jezebel. She conspired to do this. Now she'll have to face the consequences of her actions. How long to get this done, Shotgun?"

He shrugged. "Couple months at least. I'll file the paperwork, and she'll have to be formally served with your intention to annul the marriage. Then there'll be a court hearing. Since this took place in Indiana, you'll have to go back there for the hearing. You still a citizen of Vanderburgh County for tax purposes, Hope?"

"Yes." I answered reluctantly, but it wasn't like they couldn't find it out anyway. This guy, Shotgun, had found the most important part of my life in under half an hour.

"I can file it, but not until Monday. Court's closed today."

"Well," Warlock crossed his arms over his chest. "Looks like you're stuck here until we get this worked out."

"You can't be serious. You don't want me here. I no longer wish to be here. I'll sign anything I need to, but my whole life has been spent where I'm not wanted. I'm done with that."

"Of course, you can leave." Jezebel's husband stepped toward his wife and put his arm around her, kissing her temple affectionately. "But because Warlock is being an ass doesn't mean the rest of us don't want you here."

"Absolutely. Me and the other women would love to have you." Jezebel seemed genuinely warm and personable. Didn't mean I trusted any of them to have my well-being at heart. Especially since I'd been part of the reason Warlock was now married without his consent.

"I appreciate it, but I think I'll go. It'll be hard to get back to Indiana, but if you tell me when I need to go, I'll make it."

El Diablo frowned. "Where are you staying, love?"

"An apartment off Dixie Highway."

"That's not the safest area of Lake Worth." Jezebel looked up at her man. "I'd feel better if you stayed here, honey."

"You're not leaving." Warlock made the decree like he fully expected me to obey him. "Give me your address, and I'll send some prospects to get your things."

"I'm not staying here."

"Of course, you are." He gave me an insufferably superior snort. Like I was so far beneath him I wouldn't dare disobey him. It was a look I'd seen my entire life, so I knew it well. "Until this is taken care of, as your *husband* --" He emphasized the word and put a sneer on it for good measure. "Your safety is my responsibility."

"So, *now* you're OK with this? Make up your mind already!"

"Just so." El Diablo chuckled. "You *should* make up your mind, Warlock."

Warlock gave him a withering look, but El Diablo laughed again. Then Warlock declared, "I *have* made up my mind. She stays here until Shotgun and Wrath get this marriage thing taken care of. Until then, I will do my duty and see she's taken care of."

"I'm not a *duty*," I spat. "I have no idea why Mrs. Wagner thought this was a good idea, but it's obvious she underestimated the degree of asshole you really are. I'm leaving."

"Try it," Warlock said with a grin. "See how far you get." That sexy smirk on his face was the last straw.

He turned away from me, dismissing me. Mrs. Wagner had been the only person I'd ever met who'd talked to me and treated me as an equal. Like I had something to offer the world besides being a burden on everyone. He said the word "husband" like it was nothing more than my permission for him to control me. like everyone else had always done. Used me until I had nothing left to offer, then discarded me like trash. To me, the word "husband" represented the start of something I'd longed for my entire life. Stability. A family. Mutual respect, if not love.

When he dismissed me like an errant child sent to her room, it was all I could take. I snagged a full bottle of Woodford Reserve sitting on the bar and swung it at his head with a battle cry.

Surprisingly, the bottle didn't break. Warlock dropped to his knees before collapsing completely to the floor. Almost immediately he tried to push himself up, shaking his head to clear it. Down but not out.

"Ohmigod!" I thought that was Jezebel, but it might have been the other woman. "You *go*, girl!"

"Leave him." El Diablo said. "He dug this grave. Let him wallow in it." He turned to me. "Come, sweet Hope. Jezebel will set you up in a room and make sure you're comfortable with everything you need. You'll be our honored guest while you're here."

Jezebel put her arm around my shoulders while El Diablo took the bottle from my hands. He winked at me but said nothing else. The two women took me deeper into the clubhouse, leading me to a spacious suite.

"Did you bring anything with you, sweetheart?" Jezebel asked the question gently. I had the feeling she saw more than I wanted her to see.

"Yeah." I indicated my large bag. "Everything I own is in here. I came expecting to stay with Maximilian... er, Warlock. And I didn't really like the place I was staying at." I shuddered slightly. "It gets scary at night."

Jezebel pursed her lips. "That won't do at all. Esther, I think we need to go shopping."

Esther grinned. "I'll get the club credit card. Girls' day out?"

"Of course! Get the other ol' ladies together. We'll leave in an hour."

"What's happening?" I got the feeling I was being stiff-armed into doing what these women wanted, but they were being so nice, I didn't want to seem ungrateful.

"We're all going shopping!" Esther clapped her hands. "You'll absolutely love the other women here." She checked her watch. "It's early. We can still have a spa day. See if you can get El Diablo to contact the Royal and have them stay open a little late for us. He knows the shops we like. We can go to the spa there, so we won't be too late."

"Great idea! Hope, unpack your things and freshen up if you want. I'll round up the other women, and we'll call the girls at Salvation's Bane, too." Jezebel looked so excited by the prospect of a girls' day out, I hated to disappoint her.

"Guys, I can't go shopping."

"Why not? We got this covered, honey." Esther was as excited as Jezebel.

"This is embarrassing, but I don't have money

for shopping. I don't mind tagging along, but I'm on a very limited budget."

"Pfft." Jezebel waved me off. "None of us pay for anything around here. That's why we have a club card."

"I can't let you do that. I don't want to feel like I'm taking advantage of your kindness."

Both women laughed. "Honey, you're not taking advantage of anything. Besides, you can't stop us. Even if you decide not to enjoy the day with us, we're still bringing you back a whole bunch of stuff. At least if you go with us, you know you'll love what we buy."

"I coldcocked a member of the club. Why isn't anyone angry over that?"

Jezebel shrugged. "He deserved it. Besides, Warlock has had it coming since he got here. Liam -- er -- El Diablo says he's going to be a fantastic asset for Black Reign, but he's an arrogant asshole. We had a running bet on who would slug him first."

"Uh-huh." Esther picked up the narrative. "Shotgun thought it would be Noelle. Lottie said Samson was betting on himself."

"I'd forgotten about that! He's gonna be bummed." Jezebel grinned.

"I still think I should leave. It'd be better for all concerned."

"Not for us. We haven't had the chance to get to know you." Esther smiled warmly at me. "And not for you. Give us a chance to convince you to stay. Please?"

How could anyone say no to these women? I had learned to read when people were disingenuous and only trying to appease me until they could get me out of their hair. I didn't detect that here.

I was glad I went with them. It was the best time I'd ever had. The trip was supposed to be a shopping trip for everyone. There were a dozen women from two clubs and at least twice that many men. It was like a show of solidarity. And maybe that was exactly what it was. The bikers and their women didn't try to hide who they were. The women all wore vests with the words, "Property of" and the name of their man with their club emblem in the center. The men had similar vests with their club name and city they hailed from as well as the club emblem. They all wore them proudly. I was the only one in the group who didn't look like they belonged. Story of my life.

They took me to a day spa and hair and nail salon. The stylist chastised me for trying to cover us such a "gorgeous" natural color. Flaming orange wasn't what I'd call flattering, but the man worked some magic and managed to bleach out the black, or something, and match up my natural color. I had to admit, I liked looking in the mirror and seeing the correct reflection looking back at me. I'd dyed my hair in an effort to blend in. It hadn't worked.

Noelle, a woman who I'd found out had trained to be an MMA fighter, had hair a lighter shade than mine. When the stylist was done with me, she high-fived me and declared us "sisters from another mister."

When we returned to the clubhouse, I was all smiles but completely exhausted. As far as I could tell, the only clothing anyone had bought had been for me. Oh, the women made a fuss out of trying stuff on, but when it came to purchasing items, the stuff they'd helped me pick out seemed to be the only things leaving the stores in bags.

Esther and Jezebel stayed with me once the other women had helped carry all my things into the room they'd given me. Each hugged me. Jezebel handed me a phone.

"This has all our numbers in it. If you need anything, you call or text. We'll make sure you're good and decide how to proceed. No matter what it is, Hope. Especially if Warlock makes a pest of himself. You'll have to face him sooner or later, but we and our men all have your back. You're one of us."

"Until I'm not," I said softly, already missing the companionship these women had shown me, something I'd never really had before. Not like this.

"You'll always be one of us." Esther had been the one I'd gravitated to the most. She was more reserved, but I thought she might have had as strict an upbringing as I had. It was something about the way she conducted herself. Always reserved. Always unfailingly polite. Also, anytime someone swore, she blushed almost scarlet. "You might have come here for Warlock, but, right now, you belong more to us than you do to him. You decide he's not worth the trouble, we've still got your back."

"Always, honey." Jezebel nodded at the phone once again. "Call. I find out you needed us and kept it to yourself, I'll use my power as the president's ol' lady to put you on Elf duty during the Christmas party."

That perked me up. "Christmas party? What's Elf duty?"

The girls grinned at each other before Jezebel answered me. "You'll find out. We start decorating for it tomorrow. It's a tradition I started when I first came here nine years ago."

"The guys get into it, though they pretend they hate it, and we get all the community children involved."

"Especially those in group homes with no families of their own." When Jezebel said this, my breath caught.

"You mean, you invite orphaned and abandoned children here for a Christmas party?" Surely I'd misunderstood. That couldn't possibly be what they meant.

"Of course! Liam and I adopted our daughter after the first party."

"It's hard to believe that was nine years ago." Esther smothered a yawn. "I'm sorry. This baby seems to take more out of me than the first two." She rubbed her tummy. "I promised Shotgun I wouldn't overdo it." She grinned. "I may have overdone it."

"Well, I'm not pregnant," I said with a chuckle, "but I know what you mean. You guys wore me out. But I had a really good time. Thank you for making me feel so welcome."

"Good." Jezebel grinned. "We did our job properly. I'll come get you for breakfast tomorrow. You're welcome to explore the clubhouse and grounds if you like, but a word of warning. The club girls can be a might territorial with the unattached men. Warlock is new so they're still fighting over him. If you're serious about letting him go, it's not a big deal. But, if you think you might want to keep him, shut down any advances they make on him immediately."

"I think I'm good. If I didn't love his mother so much, I'd find him and smother him in his sleep."

"Now, that's what I'm talkin' about." Jezebel gave me a big hug. "You're gonna fit in around here perfectly."

"Good night!" Esther waved as she and Jezebel left, shutting the door behind them.

I was exhausted. Happy, but exhausted. Well, except now I had visions of Warlock surrounded by women. Damned man. Why did he have to be the sexiest man I'd ever seen when I was nothing more than a nobody? Always had been. Even once I was out on my own, I'd never found a place I fit in. I was too different with too different a background from everyone else I'd ever met. Even the other children where I'd grown up hadn't had as much trouble moving on with their lives as I had after they left the home. We were all messed up in one way or another. No kid could grow up in the system and not be messed up. But I seemed to be more trouble than I was worth to everyone I'd ever met.

Well, to everyone other than Mrs. Wagner.

I missed her so much. thinking about her brought tears to my eyes. She was the only person who ever understood me, and even she admitted I wasn't the type of person she'd have ever befriended if she'd been healthy. She'd said she would have missed out on a beautiful friend. It was the only time I'd ever doubted what she'd told me. I think I was her last resort. She was difficult to the staff, having been used to having things a certain way. Life in a nursing home had been a huge adjustment for her. I was the only one who put up with her. I grew to love her so much. I thought I understood her better than about anyone else. She understood me as much as anyone could, I suppose.

Which was why I wanted to believe the fairytale she presented with her son. Sure, he was way older than me, but she'd said I needed a strong, wise man to take care of me, because she could see I was going to cause beautiful chaos wherever I went. Now, I realized no one wanted that kind of responsibility. Not for someone like me. No one ever had. No one ever would.

The sacks of clothing and personal items the girls

had picked out and bought for me were epic. I had so much stuff, there was no way I could go through it tonight. I was dog-tired. I wanted to wrap my hair in a towel and go to sleep. While it looked wonderful, it stank something fierce. It was why I'd put off touching up the roots. Well that, and I didn't want to spend the money on hair color. Even the at-home stuff was money I didn't need to waste, let alone what the women had spent on me.

I looked at the mountain of stuff and could have cried. For multiple reasons. Shame at not being able to purchase it myself. Gratitude. Hope. Guilt.

With a sigh, I changed my mind, starting to go through everything and put it away neatly. If they could spend so much money on me, the very least I could do was take care of it properly.

Once it was all done, I was barely able to stay upright. I got two towels. One to wrap my hair in, one to lay over the pillow for when the towel slipped as I slept. Then I crawled under the covers and promptly passed out.

Chapter Three
Warlock

I was going to hell. In a handbasket. Over the weekend, it didn't matter where I was or what I was doing, I managed to catch glimpses of Hope everywhere. She was usually with one of the ol' ladies, but occasionally I'd see her by herself. Usually sitting beside the pool, her feet dangling in the water. She never got in. Just sat on the edge.

When she'd come back from her shopping trip with the women, seeing her with the proper hair color had almost been more than I could take. She was heartbreakingly lovely yet awkward as hell. She tried too hard to please everyone. It was like she had no idea how to interact with others without being told what to do. Or was constantly expecting to be kicked out of the group. That thought didn't sit well with me.

This whole situation with Hope was so fucking fishy, it stank like three-day-old roadkill in July. What had my mother been up to?

"You know, you could try apologizing to the girl." El Diablo stood by my side as I watched her playing with one of the many Saint Bernard dogs bounding around the compound. Who the fuck had so many fucking huge dogs?

"She's the one trying to manipulate me. Not the other way around."

"You don't know that. Seems to me she's even more caught up in this than you are." El Diablo braced his forearms on the railing where we stood on the balcony above the compound yard. "Shotgun and Wrath have been looking into her past. Perhaps you should go talk to them. Or, better yet --" He nodded toward where Hope was now laughing hysterically as three huge fucking dogs had her down on the grass licking her face as they played. "Go talk to her." He straightened. "Might shed some light on her situation. And possibly why your mother acted in the way she did."

He was right. I knew he was. "Apologizing ain't something I do well. Guess it comes from being an MC president for so long."

"You're still trying to adapt to life not being in charge of everything and everyone. You're a bit old for any advice I could give you, but let me say that, right now, you're in charge of that young woman. Maybe not how you're used to, but you're in charge of her happiness and well-being. You may not want to be her husband, but while you are, you should take it seriously. Like you alluded to before." He gripped my shoulder before clapping me on the back once. "Besides, who knows? You might find it's a role that suits you. You might find something special inside her that fulfills something inside you. Your mother apparently thought so."

"My mother wouldn't have cared about me. I can see her looking out for the girl, though. Don't make any of this right."

"No. I suppose not." El Diablo shrugged as he left me to my silent vigil.

What if I treated Hope as if she was really my wife? Not in a sexual sense, but in an affectionate sense. In a protective sense. My woman.

No. No way I could do that. I'd cared for Bev, and she'd betrayed me in every way she possibly could. She was a Goddamned spy, for Christ's sake! CI-fuckin'-A! Her mission to get information out of Argent Tech. When she couldn't get inside their security, she'd tried going through the people they knew Argent supplied. I still hadn't figured out how she knew we were involved with them. I hadn't said anything to or around her, but she could have broken my security over the years we were together. Then to find out at the end that she'd never loved me. Or even liked me, for that matter...

No. I wasn't ready for another woman in my life. After multiple years with an ol' lady, a woman I might not have completely trusted but thought I loved, I wasn't ready to take on another woman. Not even one as lovely as this one. Besides, the jury was still out on if she was crazy or not. My head was still sore where she clocked me.

Surprisingly, that memory brought a smile to my face. One thing was for sure. She had spunk. Maybe El Diablo was right. If I were honest with myself, I might have pushed my mother away intentionally. I saw the justice system fail time and time again. Heard her comment on it yet she continued to play by the system's rules. To me, not trying to fix a broken system was as bad as that system failing over and over. I might not have been able to fix it, but I was doing what I could to bring justice to my corner of the world.

OK. Fine. I'd go talk to the girl. But talk was all I'd do. I wasn't getting close to her. That would only hurt us both in the end. I'd try to find out why my mother did this and fix whatever she needed to make this easier on her.

I went back inside, descending the stairs to stroll out the front door. As I did, my phone buzzed with a text message. I looked around the yard as I pulled out my phone to read the message. That was when I spotted Razor approach Hope with a smile and a fucking wave. My gaze narrowed as the other man sat on the ground with Hope, scrubbing a hand over the head of one of the massive dogs.

Oh, hell no!

I almost forgot about the text when my phone buzzed again. Unlocking the screen, I glanced down. Shotgun had the necessary paperwork ready to file for the annulment process. He was waiting for my go-ahead.

I glanced up at Hope and Razor. And stuck my fucking phone back in my pocket without replying.

"No. I've never had a dog of my own." Hope sounded unsure of herself. Nervous. "I always thought I wanted a cat."

"We'll see what we can do about that." Razor grinned as he continued to rough up the ears of the giant dog sitting next to them. The dog looked like he adored the attention. Hope mimicked his actions with the other mutt. One would think she'd never petted a dog before.

"There's no wrong way to do it, you know." Razor spoke gently. Like he was afraid of spooking the young woman.

Hope looked down, snatching her hand from the dog. The overgrown mutt whined and lay beside her, putting his head in her lap and looking up at her like the only thing in the world he wanted was for her to continue petting him.

"I'm not used to animals," she admitted softly.

"So? Get used to them. They'll let you know if they want you to do something different. See how he's telling you he wants you to continue petting him?"

"I-I... yeah. I guess he does."

"If he doesn't like what you're doing, he'll walk away or move so you're petting him where he wants. He's not gonna get mad at you. He wants you to like him. Most domestic animals do." Then Razor grinned.

"Cats, though. Well, it's more like they tolerate you. Once they're grown, anyway. Kittens are different."

Hope graced Razor with the most beautiful smile I'd ever seen. She still seemed hesitant, but relieved Razor had explained things to her. Who had to do that? Explain to an adult how to pet an animal.

"Thank you, Razor." She looked down at the dog while she continued to pet his head, ruffing up his ears. The dog looked like he was in heaven. "For explaining without making fun of me."

"Honey, ain't no one gonna make fun of you around here. They do, you come find me and I'll bust up a motherfucker."

"I'm not... that is, I've never been around animals much."

Razor shrugged. "Not everyone has. It's nothing to worry over. Anything in this compound is OK to pet. We wouldn't let unfriendly animals or animals that didn't like people around the children."

"I appreciate you telling me."

"Now. How about a ride? I'll take you to the best restaurant in Palm Beach. Tito makes a mean burger, and Marge makes the best milkshakes."

"Excuse the fuck outta me!" I'd had all I could take. Not only was Hope breaking my heart, there was no way in hell Razor was putting her on the back of his bike.

Razor smirked at me. "Hey there, Warlock." The big man lay back on one elbow where he sat next to Hope.

"You tryin' to make a move on my wife?"

Razor barked out a laugh, like this whole situation was the height of hilarity. "Last I heard you were getting your marriage annulled. I'd say that makes her fair game. Takin' her to Tito's. See if I can get Marge to help me get into Hope's good graces."

"Fuckin' marriage ain't annulled yet. Until then, she's still my wife. Lay the fuck off."

Hope shrunk in on herself, as if trying to disappear. I felt like a complete ass. But, Goddamnit, she was *my* wife. Not Razor's.

Razor chuckled. "Go to hell, Warlock. You might have been president of your old club, but you ain't shit here. I saw what happened when Hope first got here. You might not want her in your life, but that don't mean no one does. Besides, you can't expect the girl to put her life on hold while you tear apart a marriage that obviously meant something to her." Razor said the last with an even more disapproving growl than he had the rest of his speech. I got it but wasn't sure I was ready to admit it yet.

"I can and I will. Until Shotgun and Wrath work their magic, she's still legally my wife. By her own doing."

"I'm gonna go." Hope gently pushed the dog off her lap and stood. "Thanks for the offer, Razor. But I think I'll stay here this evening."

"Honey, don't let him bully you into doing what he wants." Razor stood and put himself solidly between me and Hope. It was a move I didn't like. At all. I wanted nothing between us. "You want to go with me, you let me handle this bastard."

"He's not a bastard." All of a sudden, Hope's chin quivered like she was fighting not to cry. "His mother and father were married for forty-nine years. She was eighteen when she married. Nineteen when she had Warlock. But they were married."

"Bad choice of words, honey. I know you loved his mother."

"I did." Her voice was soft, and I could see a tear

slip from her sparkling emerald eyes. "She was the mother I --" She stopped abruptly, clearing her throat. "Thanks for the offer, Razor. But I think I'll go to my room."

Before I could stop her, Hope turned and sprinted toward the clubhouse, the dog she'd been playing with hot on her heels.

I turned to face Razor. When I did, his fist met my face. Hard. Once again, I found myself struggling to stay upright. All because of a slip of a girl who'd married me without my knowledge.

"Mother fuck." I shook it off, glaring at Razor. "That's your free one, mate. Next person to take a shot at me better knock me the fuck out or be ready for a fuckin' fight."

"Bring it any time, you son of a bitch. I realize your situation is less than ideal, but Hope is a sweet, innocent, very insecure young woman. If you don't want her, don't be surprised if more of the men here besides me take an interest. The right man takes her in, you'll have more than a fight on your hands, because that girl is *absolutely* worth fighting for. You win her heart she'll be yours for life. She won't stray. She won't do anything to betray you. Why? Because she's *starved* for positive attention. She gets what she needs, and you'll see her thrive. I for one would love to see the kind of woman she could become."

Razor spat on the ground at my feet before stalking off. Tank and Iron met him, and the three conversed for a few seconds before continuing on into the main compound.

Fuck! I had no idea what to do. Had no idea what I wanted. I took out my phone and stared at Shotgun's text for a full minute before tucking the phone back into my pocket. I'd form a reply later.

Right now, I needed to figure out a way to fix this. I might not want to be married to Hope, but it was obvious she'd cared for my mother, and I was grateful. It hadn't been me who'd cut ties with my mother, but I was glad she'd had someone who cared for her before she died. Hell, I hadn't even known she'd passed away. This was so fucked up.

* * *

Hope

I had to get out of here. This was the worst idea in the history of ideas. Mrs. Wagner meant the world to me. I'd believed she knew what she was doing, but it was obvious she'd either misjudged her son, or she really was using me to try to make his life miserable, like he'd implied. Was that the real truth of the whole situation? Had she used me to get back at her son? The thought made me sick to my stomach.

I barely made it into my room and to the bathroom before I skidded to my knees in front of the toilet and puked. Tears streamed down my face, dripping into the toilet as I heaved over and over. Before I realized it, I was sobbing uncontrollably. Mrs. Wagner had been the mother I'd never had. The one person in my life who gave a damn about me. Had she betrayed me in the worst possible way? Was I really not worth anything more than for people to use as a sacrificial lamb?

"It's gonna be OK, baby." The male voice was calm. Almost tender. He sounded familiar, but my mind wouldn't go there. A hand pulled my hair back and held it carefully out of the way while I vomited one last time. Somewhere close I heard the high-pitched whine of a dog. The toilet flushed, and a damp cloth was wiped gently over my face as I was urged away from the commode to sit back. I thought I was in someone's arms, but I wasn't sure. My vision was blurred with tears, and I was too overwhelmed to really care. "Let it out if you need to. I'm here and I ain't goin' nowhere."

"I j-just w-wanna go h-home." I continued to cry. Grieve.

"Tell me where that is and I'll get you there."

I shook my head. "She's gone. I c-can't get b-back." Voicing Mrs. Wagner's death out loud, no matter how reserved the form, brought a fresh flood of sharp grief. Before her, I'd never had anyone to lose. The time I'd spent with her had been the happiest of my life. I helped with her care. I talked with her endlessly. We shared stories. She'd actually cared about me. At least I'd thought she had. What if all that had been one more way someone had manipulated me? What if the one person in the whole world I'd grown to love hadn't loved me back?

"We'll figure this out, honey. Just breathe for me. Let it out if you need to, but I need you to breathe."

On some level, I knew he was right. I wasn't breathing like I needed to because of the great sobs racking my body. All the grief I'd tried so hard to suppress crashed down on me, and there was no way to escape it.

I took a big gulp of air, letting it out in a wail of grief. I had no idea how long I sat there, but the arms around me never let go. The soft words of promise never stopped. Occasionally, the man would wipe my face gently before wrapping me up tightly in his arms again.

When the storm had finally passed, I took a tentative peek up at my comforter.

Warlock...

With a gasp, I tried to pull away. He frowned down at me and growled, tightening his grip.

"Let me up."

"No."

He continued to hold me, rocking slightly. I wanted to protest. I really did. But the sensation was so foreign, so... *welcomed*, all I could do was sit there in his arms and soak it all up like a sponge.

As the time went by, he didn't make a move to release me, and I didn't dare move in case he took that as his cue to let me up. Like I'd told him to do. Because, now, I really didn't want him to let me up. I trembled in his arms, tears still leaking from my eyes down my cheeks. Warlock was the last link I had to Mrs. Wagner. The only link I had to the one person I considered family.

As expected, Warlock finally shifted me to the floor beside him. Surprisingly, when he stood, he bent and scooped me up. Back into his arms.

"You don't have to do this." At least my voice was steady now. I was sure I looked a mess. A pretty crier I was not. "I can walk. Nothing wrong with my legs."

"I know." He continued to walk to the bed and sat, swinging his legs around so he sat with his back against the headboard, his booted feet hanging off the edge at the ankle, with me sitting sideways in his lap.

I expected him to say something, to break the spell weaving around us, but he didn't. He sat there, me wrapped in his arms, his chin resting on top of my head.

At some point, I dozed off. When I woke to a darkened room, I was alone in the middle of the bed. A blanket was tucked securely around me and the bathroom light was on, the door left open a crack so I could see if I needed to get up.

I sat up, looking around with a sigh. It was expected, but more disappointing than I thought it would be. A big dog, the one I'd been playing with, lay next to me. He whined softly, scooting closer so he could lay his huge head in my lap and looked up at me with sad eyes.

"At least you're still with me, buddy." I rubbed his head. His tail thumped softly on the bed.

"Still here, girl." Warlock shifted from his seat in a chair next to the bed. He was in the darkest corner of the room, which was why I hadn't noticed him right away. He should have startled me but instead I felt a surge of relief. "Wasn't gonna leave you alone after you bein' so upset."

"I'm fine." It was an automatic answer. If I were honest, I really wasn't fine. I missed Mrs. Wagner and hated that feeling of being all alone again.

"Are not. About shit like this, you're a fuckin' awful liar."

"Are you always so abrasive?" I wanted to push Warlock away. Not only had he seen me at my worst, but I still needed to lick my wounds before I was ready to face him again.

"Nope. I'm usually worse. I'm making an effort for you."

I snorted. "I'd hate to see what you're normally like."

"You ready to talk?"

"I assume your people have the annulment process started." I shrugged. "I don't really see any reason to talk unless there are things you need me to do. Do I need to go back to Indiana now?"

"No." His tone was soft, but his answer succinct. I wasn't sure which question he'd answered.

When he said nothing else, I sat still, afraid to move. I knew he didn't like me, but I wanted to be in his presence as long as he'd allow it. It was pathetic, but I couldn't help myself. Especially after earlier. Being in his arms had made something inside me shift. For the first time since Mrs. Wagner had passed away, I felt hope. For happiness. For a sense of belonging. For a happy, fulfilling future.

"Tell me what happened between you and my mother."

"Not much to tell. I helped her. She grew to like me." I sniffed, tears threatening. After my earlier release of emotions, I was better able to hold on to them.

"I'd say there was quite a bit to tell." He leaned forward, the light from the bathroom spilling over his face. He didn't look like he pitied me or was angry with me. He looked genuinely curious. And determined. "My mother didn't like being in the presence of people she didn't consider equal. That tells me you were special to her. She saw something in you that she believed worth her time."

"I doubt it was as complicated as all that. I was kind to her. She was kind to me. I think she was as lonely as I was and we... I don't know. *Fit*."

"My mother was never lonely. And if she was, it was because she drove people away from her on purpose." He leaned his forearms on his knees, lacing his fingers. "You loved her." It wasn't a question.

"I did," I answered softly.

"Why?"

The question caught me off guard. "Because she was good to me."

"Did she love you?"

"I have no idea." This time, my answer was

barely a whisper. It was that question that had driven me over the edge.

"Why do you think she did this? Married us."

"All I know is what I told you before. She wanted you happy."

"And what about you? Did she take into account your happiness?" I wished I could see his face clearly. The light from the bathroom spilled across him, but there was too much shadow to see his features to read him.

"She knew I'd be happy if I could make you happy enough for you to stay with me."

He shook his head. "That doesn't make sense. You'll have to explain."

"My past is my own business, Warlock." I'd sound too pathetic if I explained my past to him.

"We're married, Hope. My wife can't have secrets from me."

"Our marriage is going to be annulled. There's no reason --"

"Ain't annulled yet. Give me a reason why I should let it stand."

I wasn't naive enough to think he was asking a question I had a choice in answering. This was a man demanding answers and expected to get them. Mrs. Wagner had told me he was the most stubborn person she'd ever met. Except maybe for herself.

"I can't."

"Yes, you can. Talk to me, Hope. You obviously wanted a husband. You have one. Treat me like one and talk to me. That's the only way this works."

"You're confusing me. I thought you didn't want a wife."

"Pretend I do." He sounded so reasonable. I knew it was foolish, and I was probably acting too stupid to live, but I found it easy to pretend.

"Pretending is what I'm best at."

"Then tell me, Hope. What happened between you and my mother?"

"She… I don't know. Adopted me? She said I was the daughter she never had. She said I was God's second chance for her to do right by her son and that, maybe, by doing right by you she could do right by me, too."

"Good. Now tell me the rest."

"This isn't easy to tell, Warlock."

"Call me Max. My mother always called me Maximilian, but I'm not a Maximilian. Max."

"All right. Max, then." I cleared my throat.

"Wait. I'll be right back." He stood and left the room. I breathed a sigh of relief. Maybe he'd changed his mind. No such luck. He returned less than five minutes later with two bottles of water. He opened one and handed it to me before opening the other for himself. "Now. Talk to me, Hope. I know firsthand my mother isn't an easy woman to love. Tell me why you loved her so much."

I sighed. Might as well get this first part out. It was kind of like taking off a Band-Aid. If I did it quickly, it wouldn't hurt as badly. "I was an abandoned child. From birth. I was left with the sisters at a Catholic group home. When that happens, if no one comes to claim the child, the sisters name it. They named me Hope. My last name, Hamilton, came from the county I was born in. Not in Indiana, but Ohio. As I got older, the group home where I lived became hopelessly overcrowded. Because my guardian was set up through the Catholic organization and I was easy to move because I was older and understood what was happening, I got transferred to a home in Evansville."

"If you were abandoned as an infant, why weren't you adopted out? Isn't it easier for a baby to be adopted than an older child?"

"I'm sure it is. But I was sick. Apparently, I was hooked on meth from birth. I spent about two months in a neonatal ICU going through detox. After that, there were developmental delays. I guess not many prospective parents are willing to take on a baby like that. At least --" I shrugged, trying to act if it didn't matter to me one way or the other when it was deeply shameful and painful for me to think about. "-- No one was willing to take me on."

I was silent for a while. Telling this was harder than I'd expected. "Can we do this another time? I don't --"

"We're doing it now, honey. How can I make the telling easier?"

Yeah. I wasn't touching that one. "You can't. Other than not making me tell it?"

He stood, taking a long pull of his water. I could feel him watching me. When he set the bottle on the nightstand, he nodded at mine. "Drink." I did, the cold water soothing to my dry throat. Dry from sleep. Raw from the crying I'd done earlier.

When I finished, he reached for it, setting it on the nightstand next to his. Then he sat on the bed next to me. I realized that he no longer wore his jeans and motorcycle boots, but soft, cotton pants and a T-shirt. Instead of merely sitting next to me, he pulled me into his lap, like I'd sat before after my bout of grief.

"There." He tightened his arms around me. "You seemed to like it before."

"It's nice," I whispered.

"Good." He squeezed once, then kissed the top of my head before resting his chin there. "Now. Tell me, Hope."

"There's not much to tell, really. I was struggling in school, not that anyone cared. All they wanted was for me to pass with the minimum. It didn't matter if I did well, I just had to pass. It was embarrassing to always be in the slow classes. It's not supposed to be differentiated, but kids know. Special reading. Special math. Basics were difficult. Not because I didn't understand it, though. I had trouble putting it on paper. I could solve out loud any math problem they put in front of me. I could read but answering questions about what I read was hard. I knew the answers if they read it out loud to me, but it all got messed up going from my brain to my hands or something.

"Anyway, the sisters decided I needed to prepare for life outside of the home. I had to be able to hold down a job so I could have a place to live. When I was thirteen, they got me a job after school as a volunteer at one of the nursing homes the church had. I passed out magazines or books. Talked with the residents there. Played games with them. Helped them eat if they had difficulty. Helped them to the bathroom. That kind of thing. I met your mother my second week there."

"How long did you work there?"

"I volunteered until I turned sixteen. Then I worked until your mother died two weeks ago."

"Why didn't you contact me when she passed? Or better yet, why didn't the nursing home?" He didn't sound angry, but I thought he might be a bit hurt that he hadn't known.

"I didn't contact you because I didn't have a way to. She didn't say anything about having your phone number. Just told me where you'd be."

"I've only been here a month, Hope. Until then, I

was in Evansville."

"I know. She told me your son, Aiden, knew where you were and would help me get to you."

"Why didn't Aiden call me?"

"Because Mrs. Wagner told him not to. When I came to him, he tried to tell me it wasn't a good idea. He said you'd been through a rough time recently and wouldn't welcome me like I was expecting."

"He was right. Did he tell you what happened?"

"No. He said it was your story." The more we talked, the more relaxed I became. I found myself snuggling against him. I couldn't help myself. He was warm and felt safe. Even if he'd been a dick to me before, for whatever reason, he wasn't being one now. And I loved this feeling.

"So, you worked for the nursing home after you graduated high school." He was trying to get me back on track, and I let him, figuring it was best to get it out now that I'd started.

"I did. I couldn't pass my CNA test, but I worked hard and they let me stay. I'd had the schooling, I just couldn't pass the test. They were short-staffed. There was some kind of loophole they used in the new regulations for nursing homes and the hiring of staff. They kept me on, but I got paid less than I would have if I'd been an actual CNA." I shrugged. "I didn't mind. I made enough to pay for the government housing apartment and to eat. And working there meant I got to spend time with Mrs. Wagner."

"You keep calling her Mrs. Wagner. Why didn't you call her Verna? That was her first name."

"Out of respect, I guess. I think it was what first caught her attention. I never called the residents by their first name. I used their last names and Mr. or Mrs. It was the way I'd been raised. I mean, if one ever called Sister Mary Catherine Mary, or Catherine, the consequences were dire."

He chuckled lightly. "Yes, I supposed it would be. I could see my mother liking the formality of that."

"It wasn't formality. It was genuine respect. For all the residents. They'd seen so much in their lives, and I loved hearing their stories. It was like I got to live another life. One where I had a family."

"So that's the real reason you were agreeable to do what she asked. Wasn't it?"

The shame of it all was nearly too much. "I realize it was playing with your life, Max. I'm really sorry. It's... she dangled something in front of me I wanted with all my heart. I knew it was ludicrous, but she was so sure you'd welcome me with open arms. That, if I tried hard enough, I could make you happy enough to want me in your life."

Warlock sighed. The name suited him more than Max or even Maximilian. "OK. You told me what brought you to this point in life. Let me tell you about me. Why this isn't something I welcome. We'll talk it out and decide what to do next. Together. Can you do that?"

"Of course."

"Good." He shifted his position. It brought me a bit closer to him. When I moved one arm around his neck, he seemed to like the new position. It let me rest my head on his shoulder while he talked.

Chapter Four
Warlock

In my experience, women were all about manipulation. They manipulated you with their vulnerability or with sex to get what they wanted. I knew it sounded misogynistic, but that had been my experience. This girl, however...

Maybe she was playing me. She wanted a family or to be loved or whatever. But why? Why choose me? If her story was to be believed -- and I thought it might be -- then she was as much a victim of my mother's meddling as I was. Maybe more, because she had no idea she was being manipulated. It had only recently occurred to her that my mother might have had less than honorable intentions when she set this whole situation in motion. Hope had voiced it in the middle of her grief. I doubt the girl even realized she'd said anything. Her tale had obviously been very painful for her. The least I could do was give her my own story of heartache.

"I was with my ol' lady for seven years. She came to me with a daughter from a previous relationship. Bev was clingy and very jealous if my attention wasn't focused squarely on her, so I tried my best to protect Chloe while keeping my distance. For the most part, Bev sent Chloe away to boarding schools anyway, so I didn't have to worry about being careful of any kind of relationship with the girl. I was president of the MC I belonged to, so sometimes we had heated arguments about the time I spent away from her and with the club. The conflicts were such a strain that most of the time, I alleviated her jealousy by taking her with me to the clubhouse instead of going alone. I had no idea at the time, but I was playing right into her hands."

In a way, admitting all this to Hope was cathartic. I was examining my relationship with Bev for what it really was. And the more I thought about it, the more and more I was questioning my reasons for wanting Bev with me at the time.

"I can't go into detail about what she wanted from me, but suffice it to say, Iron Tzars has connections envied by many people. Governments. Bev was trying to get information about those connections."

"Must be some pretty good connections if she tried for seven years."

I couldn't help but grin. My girl might have some issues in school, but she wasn't unintelligent. "You'd be correct. Looking back, I think she tried to call it quits several times, but the carrot dangled in front of her handlers was too great. So she stayed. Most of it I didn't find out until a couple of weeks ago."

"You loved her." It wasn't a question. "I can see how what I went along with would make you angry. I'm so sorry, Warlock."

"Max."

She looked up at me. "Warlock suits you better."

"Warlock's the biker, Hope. He's not an easy man."

"You are who you are. You shouldn't have to hide it. Not for anyone. Especially not me."

That surprised me. El Diablo had been right. I'd needed this talk with Hope. "You're proving to be a source of surprises. The insight you have about life and people is refreshing and not something I'd expect in a woman your age."

"Where is your wife, Warlock? You obviously loved her."

I was silent for a long time, thinking about my answer carefully. Neither question had easy answers.

"I didn't mean to pry," she said softly, stiffening in my arms. She tried to get up, but I tightened my hold on her. My lips rested on the top of her forehead. Her skin was soft, and I couldn't help but kiss her. I wanted to do more than that, but all I had to do was continue this conversation to remind myself why doing more with this girl was the worst idea.

"You didn't, honey. I'm trying to be as honest as I can. Because I'm coming to realize I've not been honest with myself. Just give me a minute here."

She did, not saying another word. Instead, she snuggled farther into my shoulder until she buried her face in my neck. She inhaled covertly, but deeply. Bev had never done that. If anything, she'd hated the way I smelled because there was always a bit of a gasoline scent clinging to me from the time I spent on my bike. Did Hope like what she found? I'd have to pay attention. Assuming she didn't run screaming from the room after my confession.

"Bev." I sighed heavily. "No. We weren't married. To my club, her being my ol' lady was the same as being married, but I never made it official. Never even asked her to marry me. Probably because I knew she wouldn't have done it. As to the question of did I love her? I thought I did. So much so I let her effectively take my club from me."

"Your club means a lot to you."

"It does. It did. I have no idea if my relationship with them can ever be repaired. Probably not. My son is now president, so I've lost him, too. All because I let Bev manipulate me."

"You see what I did as manipulative. And you'd be right." Again, she tried to move. Again, I held her fast.

"Shh." I kissed her forehead again. I had to watch that. The show of affection would only endear me to her more than she already was, and I had no plans on staying in her life. "Let me finish. Bev's dead."

She gasped. "I'm so sorry."

"Don't be. She deserved what she got." I took a breath. "I resigned as president. My son was voted in. Bev argued with me violently over this. She didn't want me to give up my position in the club, because it made her chances of getting the information she needed even less than it had been before. When I steadfastly refused to reverse my decision, she talked me into convincing my son to take on her daughter as his ol' lady. Sting was never going to agree to that, and I knew it. But we both went through the motions.

"Chloe split. Went to find her father at another club, this one in Kentucky. Bones MC. After hearing her tale, Bones reached out to Iron Tzars. Sting took a few men, myself included, to Bones territory to make sure Chloe was good. Turned out she'd been taken in by a member of Bones who'd made her his ol' lady. She was happy and had no desire to leave. Bev took exception. Tried to kill the girl. Shot the girl's father by accident when he jumped in front of her to take the bullet."

"Oh no!"

"He's fine. So's Chloe," I tried to reassure her. Even though she didn't know any of these people, her empathy seemed genuine. She looked up at me with such distress, I believed her. Then I remembered I'd believed Bev too. "Apparently, Bev had tried to have the same arrangement with Sword -- Chloe's father -- as she'd had with me. Every single man there knew there was no way either of our clubs would ever be safe as long as Bev was still alive. Since she was my ol' lady, I took the responsibility."

"You killed her?" Now, there was fear in Hope's eyes. She stiffened in my arms once again. This time, I didn't restrain her. If she wanted up, I'd let her go. Surprisingly, she stayed where she was. continued to look up at me, waiting for an answer.

"I did. She knew death was her sentence, though she thought it would happen later and, likely, that she could talk me out of turning her over to the club. I made it quick and didn't tell her it was coming. But yes. I killed her. My woman. My responsibility."

She was silent for a long moment before nodding her head. "That's a warning to me. Isn't it?"

"It is, honey."

"What would I have to do? You know. For you to kill me?"

"Betray my club. Understand me -- my club is my family. Right now, I'm here. I'm still the outsider, but Black Reign is doing its best to take me in and treat me like family. I'm a member, but I've only been here a month. I'm useful to El Diablo, so he's done things much faster than he should have. Given my history -- which he knows from beginning to end -- your presence here under the circumstances you brought with you is being looked at carefully. Don't think I want anything to happen to you, Hope. I don't. You seem like a girl caught up in my mother's meddling. But, if the men here find out there's more to this story than my mother meddling in my life, if you have another reason for being here, you need to tell me now. This is your one chance to come clean. I'll mitigate the damage, sever ties, and you can go on your way provided you never come near the club again." I waited for that to sink in. "You understand?"

She nodded slightly. "I do. But I swear to you, everything I've told you is true. I've told you everything to the best of my ability. I understand why you want rid of me now. I really do."

"So, you've changed your mind? You want out of this marriage now?"

She ducked her head, and I stilled. I found myself torn as to what I wanted her answer to be. If she said yes, my problems were over. If she said no, Black Reign would continue to look into her past, digging up everything there was to know about her. She'd been here long enough, I was sure Shotgun had picked up her prints and had run them, along with facial recognition to make a positive ID. Since I'd given her this one chance to come clean, anything he found I'd make sure they didn't use against her. At least, not in the extreme. Well, not if she hadn't already betrayed Black Reign.

"I don't know. I mean, I haven't done anything like what you said and hadn't planned to. But I don't want to be where I'm not wanted." She did move off me then. I let her. She scooted to the other side of the bed and stood before walking around it to the bathroom. She shut the door behind her. I didn't hear it lock, but I was sure she had. What woman wouldn't after what I'd confessed? Was she even now calling the cops? I'd confessed to a murder.

I got up from the bed and stood by the bathroom door. Listening. At first, I heard nothing. Then there was a soft sob. Not the torrent she'd let loose earlier but more than I was comfortable with.

Gently, I tried the door. It was unlocked so I opened it, stepping inside. Immediately, she turned her back, swiping her arm over her eyes and clearing her throat to cover any sounds she'd made.

"Why are you in here? I could have been on the toilet."

I thought about lying, but why do that? I wanted her honest with me. I had to be honest with her. "Wanted to see if you'd locked yourself in here to call the police."

She turned around, her eyes wide. "Why would I do that?"

"Because I told you I killed Bev. I murdered a woman in cold blood."

"We're married. I couldn't testify against you, anyway."

"You don't *have* to testify. Doesn't mean you couldn't."

"I couldn't if you didn't want me to." She frowned. "I'm not stupid, Warlock. I paid attention in Civics class."

"I'm fully aware you're not stupid, honey. I think you've been underestimated all your life. I'm not about to make the same mistake everyone else has made about you. Though, I suspect my mother probably saw your potential. Now tell me. Why are you upset? Are you afraid of me now?"

"I should be." She looked away. Then took a breath. "You were honest with me."

"I was. I will never ask you to do something I'm not willing to do myself. I want the truth from you, so I give you the truth in return."

"Then, no. I'm not afraid of you. I realize that no matter what I do or say, you'll always believe I'm deceiving you."

"Can you blame me? I mean, I'm not a great catch, Hope. I'm surly on the best of days. Mean and hateful on the worst. I'm also thirty years your senior.

Not a great catch for a woman like you."

"A woman like me? Homeless? Penniless? Friendless? No, Warlock. To me you represent strength, safety, and stability. A man my own age could never give me that. At least, none of the ones I've met could. I knew you had a son much older than me and that you were probably set in your ways and wouldn't appreciate someone being thrust into your life. At first, I agreed to it because Mrs. Wagner asked me. I'd do anything for her, and she wanted me in your life. The more I thought about it, the more I wanted our marriage to be real. I wanted someone of my own to... I don't know. Care about what happened to me. I wanted someone to miss me if something happened to me. To leave my mark on someone's life. When I saw you --" Her voice hitched, as if she were trying to fight off tears again. Sure enough, one overflowed and tracked from each eye. She shook her head. "It doesn't matter. Just let me know what I need to do when it comes time for the paperwork."

She brushed past me and went back to the bedroom. She had her hand on the door, getting ready to leave. I knew I should let her go, but before I even knew I was going to do it, I barked out the word, "Stop!" Hope froze. "Don't leave yet. You still haven't answered my question. Do you want out of this marriage, Hope?"

"There's no right answer to that question," she said softly. "I think the better question would be do *you* want out? And I believe we both know the answer to that." She left the room, closing the door behind her.

* * *

Hope

"A little higher. To the left."

Jezebel guided me as I hung ornaments on the massive Christmas tree in the great room. It was the third time in as many days we'd gone through this same routine. On a different tree. In the same spot. Apparently, there was a mysterious Christmas bandit who made it his personal mission to ruin Christmas for everyone. The children were having an absolute ball with it. I couldn't say I wasn't having a great time, but I didn't feel like I should be there.

"Hope? Have you seen Warlock?" Esther smiled as she approached me, Shotgun at her side with his arm around her shoulders. All the couples in Black Reign seemed so happy it made my heart hurt. I wanted that for myself. I'd thought maybe Warlock was starting to see me differently after our talk, but in the end, I'd realized he wasn't looking for a reason to keep me. He was making me see how hopeless it was for me to pretend there was.

"I haven't seen him in a couple of days." I looked from Esther to Shotgun. "Do I need to go back to Indiana to receive the annulment paperwork?" I'd been dreading that news. The last thing I wanted to do was go back to Indiana alone.

Shotgun gave me a level look. "No, honey. Warlock hasn't given me the go-ahead to file it yet. I was under the impression he wanted to discuss the situation with you."

"We did. A week or so ago."

"I see. Well. I'll shoot him a text. Or have El Diablo do it."

"Yeah. I'm sorry."

"Not your fault. Warlock keeps to himself most of the time. It's not unusual for him to disappear for a few days at a time." Shotgun smiled at me. Esther gave her husband a worried look. Yeah. This wasn't awkward at all.

I turned to hang the ornament in my hand on the tree. Then I stepped back to look at it. "I think it looks better today than it did yesterday." I smiled at Jezebel. "The children made such beautiful ornaments."

"They certainly did." Jezebel stepped close, putting her arm around me.

"I don't know how you guys do it. We've been at this all morning and you're still going strong."

"Christmas is the best!" El Diablo and Jezebel's daughter, Dawn, threw her arms around her mother. The young teen was the darling of the club. From what I'd learned, the couple had adopted the girl after the first such Christmas party, organized by Jezebel. I found the club's tradition so unique and charming I wanted to be part of it. But the reminder that Warlock wasn't with me was enough to dampen my mood. After all, he was the only real tie I had to the people in Black Reign.

"I agree." I smiled brightly. "As much fun as I'm having, I think I need to take a break."

"We could all use one." Celeste was a beautiful, elegant woman. She was married to Wrath, the lawyer helping to get my marriage annulled. I felt awkward around the woman, because I always dreaded seeing her husband. "I'll see about getting some sandwich meat, bread and chips."

I waited until the women were all moving farther into the clubhouse before slipping off to go back to my room. Once the door was closed, I slumped against it, bone weary. My mind was in chaos, my heart hanging on in splintered shards. It wasn't the man, but what he represented that broke my heart the most. Warlock was larger than life to me. Unattainable. I'd realized that after our talk. Now, I found myself as alone as I had been since Mrs. Wagner's death.

With a sigh, I went to the bathroom and washed my face. The sun was bright, high in the sky. The weather warm with a cool breeze blowing off the ocean. Florida was certainly different than Indiana in winter. I could see myself enjoying the sunshine and the ocean. A sudden burst of determination hit me. because things weren't working out the way I wanted didn't mean I couldn't have a good Christmas.

I went to the dresser where I'd put all the things the women had bought me. They hadn't let me hide from the bathing suit section either, saying anyone living this close to the beach had to have a swimsuit. And yeah. One-piece wasn't in their vocabulary.

I picked out a bright green suit. The material had a metallic sheen to it, and the color complemented my skin and hair. It had a full back instead of a thong, my breasts covered by full triangles. There were ties at my neck and back, as well as at both hips. Classic string bikini, though pretty modest compared to some I'd seen since coming here. I put on a pair of shorts and a button-up linen shirt that I left unbuttoned, snagged a couple towels and shoved my feet into flip-flops before heading downstairs and outside the compound.

No one stopped me as I headed out the front walkway and across the street to the sidewalk leading to the beach entrance. Unlike most I'd seen here, this one was walled and gated, but the gate was open, and there were no signs saying it was private. The walk wasn't far, and I enjoyed it. The sun was warm on my face, and I felt my spirits lifting in the beautiful day.

The sound of the ocean waves was another first for me since coming to Florida. I'd spent my whole life with the only body of water I'd ever seen being the Ohio River, where you could see from one side to the other. I'd seen pictures and movies and news footage of various oceans before, but the reality was on a whole other level.

I stepped from the concrete to the sandy beach and moved closer to the shore. There was no one else around, and the white sand was pristine. The probability I was trespassing was high, but doing something I knew I shouldn't was oddly invigorating. Besides, if the worst thing I did was trespass on a private beach, I was sure the Sisters wouldn't have me say too many Hail Marys.

I put my towels in the sand away from the shore before walking toward the water. The sight was awe-inspiring. Sure, there were sailboats off in the distance, but there were no bridges or mountains or anything else except an impossibly blue sky. I looked down at my feet where the water rushed ashore, pulling the sand away before pushing more back only to start over again. Sure, I'd ready about this -- books were my vacation -- but to experience the reality felt even better than I imagined. A laugh burst from my chest as joy enveloped me. If nothing else positive happened while I was here, this experience, seeing the ocean and being on a beach for the very first time, was worth what it took me to get here.

Careful to not get in too deep, I waded out until the water lapped at my knees. Some waves were stronger than others, trying to push me off-balance. When that happened, I backed up a few steps. The last thing I wanted to do was lose my footing and fall, no matter how shallow the water.

I played for a little while. OK, so it was more like a couple of hours. Maybe more. I jumped waves. Sat in the shallow water and let the sand build up around me. I picked up seashells and even built a sand volcano. Which was really a cone of sand with the middle somewhat hollowed out. It collapsed halfway through, but it made me laugh. I made a note to get some buckets next time so I could make a sandcastle.

I had no idea how long I was there, but I was starting to get hungry. And very thirsty. The walk back to the compound wasn't far, but I wasn't ready to leave yet. Decision made, I went back to my towels and sat down under the sun. I was probably red as a lobster, but I didn't care. If I was sunburned, it was worth it to feel this free and, more importantly, carefree. Even for a short while.

It wasn't long before the sun did its work. I was sleepy and happy. Tucking my arms behind my head, I sighed happily. This, I could do every single day for the rest of my life. The thought had just entered my head when the sunlight suddenly dimmed, the warmth cooling in the shadow. Opening my eyes, I saw the problem.

"There a reason you're blocking my sun, Warlock?" I did my best to put all the ire I could into my voice. Given I was as mellow as a mushroom, it was damned hard.

"You're gonna burn. And you need to move back."

"Move back?"

"Yeah." The second he spoke, water tickled my feet as a wave crept up the shore.

I gasped and sat up. "I wasn't that close when I lay down!"

"I'm sure you weren't." He reached out a hand. I took it automatically, and he pulled me to my feet. "Tide's comin' in."

"Tide?" I stared at him blankly. For more than one reason. Warlock was in shorts... and nothing else.

He might be white-headed, but his body was in prime condition. The man was ripped. And had tattoos scattered over his skin in intriguing places. One snaked into the waistband of his shorts from his side, making me wonder how low on his hip it went. He was completely decent, but he represented the first man I'd been close to in this state of undress.

"Yeah, honey. Let's move your things farther up the shore, and I'll take you into the water."

Well, this was a turn. I wasn't sure I trusted this change of attitude on his part. I squinted at him, shielding my eyes from the sun. "Who are you and what have you done with Warlock?"

He snorted. "Get your shit."

I picked up the two towels and my clothes. I saw he'd set up two beach chairs and walked in that direction. He took my stuff from me, tossing it onto the chair before reaching for my hand again. He didn't wait for me to take it, just snagged my hand and led me toward the water. Then a thought occurred to me, and I stopped in my tracks.

"You're not… I mean, I didn't do anything to betray you, Warlock." If he'd decided the easiest way to get rid of his problem was to eliminate it, I was in a really bad position with no way to fight him.

"What? No!" He shook his head and, surprisingly, pulled me into his arms. "Absolutely not, Hope." I was so surprised, I let him hold me. It felt good. Damned good. Better than it had a week ago when we'd talked after my breakdown. That still embarrassed me every time I thought about it. Now, though, none of that mattered. I soaked up this rare show of affection like a sponge. And, oh, my God! He smelled *good*!

When he let me go, it was to frame my face in his

big hands and force me to look up into his eyes. What I saw there stunned me. This man was haunted. Almost immediately, he jerked his hands away and stepped back. He snagged my hand again and tugged me after him as he headed toward the ocean.

"Come on." His voice was gruff. Like his throat was tight. "Let's get in the water."

He took me much deeper than I'd gone myself. The water was past his waist, which meant it was to my chest. Waves still rolled around us, but they seemed gentler in the deeper water. As they moved our bodies, Warlock wrapped his arms around me. If I were smart, I'd have been hesitant about letting him cage me in like he was. If the man meant to kill me, I was being so stupid as to not be believed. Again, though, it felt too good to back away from him. I figured, if I was going to die, at least I'd die happy. Warlock constantly looked behind us, and it was then I remembered something I'd never really understood.

"Never turn your back on the ocean," I murmured.

"Sound advice," he said, his gaze shifting to mine before going back to the water beyond us. His lips curled slightly as if my statement amused him.

"It's just that I've always heard that expression, but never really understood what it meant. After seeing how quickly the ocean can creep up on you, I get it now."

"You didn't know the tide would come in?" He gave me a quizzical look.

"Well, I did. But I've never experienced it. I didn't even think about the way the tide would come in or when it would happen. Or even what it actually meant." I slumped my shoulders because I felt stupid. "It was an abstract thing with no context, I guess."

"I can see that. You ever been to an ocean before?"

"No." I felt defeated. I knew he was out of my league before, but this was one more thing to prove how inadequate a choice I was for a wife. No wonder the man didn't want me. It wasn't that I'd manipulated him -- or his mother had. It was so much life experience I didn't have. Things I didn't know and couldn't understand. Why would any man want a wife like me?

"I guess that makes it my job to look out for you. Seems like you were having a good time."

"I am. I love being in the sun, even though I burn. It's much better when there's water around."

"Well, this is the best swimming pool in the world. You have to be careful, and never swim alone."

"Oh, I can't swim. That's why I never got deeper than my knees." I tried to smile as I looked up at him.

He brought his full attention back to me. "You can't swim? Why didn't you say something?" Immediately, he lifted me, urging me to put my legs around his waist. At first, I was hesitant, but every time I dropped a leg, he'd use one hand to pull my thigh higher. Slowly, he made his way out of the deeper water into the shallower waves. When the water edged below my thighs, I dropped them, settling my feet on the sandy bottom. Warlock growled as he frowned down at me.

"You can't carry me out of the water like that. Someone might see!"

"Do you see anyone around here, girl?" He gave me an exasperated look.

"Well, no. But you never know!"

"This is a private beach, honey. Black Reign owns this stretch."

"But the gate was open."

"Don't matter. Everyone around here knows this is Reign's beach, and they respect it."

"I see." I really didn't. But then, if they had a bad reputation, maybe that was why people stayed away. He led me back to the chairs before snagging my shirt and putting it over my head.

"You're sunburned."

I shrugged. "Small price to pay. Won't be the first time. Doubt it will be the last." He shook his head like I was nuts before helping me into my shorts.

We walked back to the clubhouse in silence. Warlock didn't let go of my hand once. He left the chairs, saying someone would probably use them the next day. If not, he'd send a prospect to collect them. I tried to tug free a couple of times, but he ignored me and tightened his grip.

When we reached the door to my room, I expected he'd leave me there alone. Instead, he opened the door and ushered me inside. The second the door was closed, he pulled me back into his arms, burying his nose in my neck and inhaling deeply. I could feel his hard length poking my belly, and I froze.

"Warlock?"

"You smell like fuckin' sunshine and the open sea."

Instantly, my knees gave way, and I clung to his broad shoulders. "Oh, God!"

"Can't help it." His hands slid under my shirt, his big palms spreading wide to take in as much of my back as he could. "Knew you were trouble the second I laid eyes on you." When I looked up at him, he lowered his face to mine and kissed me.

If I died right this second, I wouldn't be able to regret it. I'd never been kissed before. Never been touched by a guy for any affectionate reason. The group homes I lived in separated the boys and girls, only bringing them together for meals, school, and church. I was different from most of the other kids in that they either had homes they were going back to at some point or had a high probability of being adopted or fostered out. I'd never had a home and never expected to have one after living with the Sisters my entire life. The group home was the only home I'd ever known.

Until Mrs. Wagner put the idea of me marrying her son in my head, I'd never really thought about a relationship or a family other than in the abstract. This was something similar to my surprise with the ocean. I knew a physical display of affection was involved in a relationship, but I'd never experienced it or witnessed it. It would have been overwhelming no matter what, but Warlock's kisses and touches seemed to ignite something inside me I never knew existed.

I gasped, whimpering when his tongue darted out to sweep inside my mouth. All I could do was hold on for the ride. Warlock did the driving. I did my best to follow his lead, but I had no idea what to do. In the end, I let him take what he wanted. Anything he took from me he returned ten times over. Never had I dreamed there was such pleasure in the simple act of pressing one's mouth to another's. OK, so there was nothing simple about it. He knew exactly how to use his teeth, lips, and tongue to coax the responses from me he wanted. The fact that he was so much more experienced than me should have been intimidating but was actually a comfort. He'd lead me where he wanted. And I'd follow. Willingly. Eagerly.

"Hope..." He breathed my name between kisses. It sounded almost like a prayer. Said reverently and with a longing I thought rivaled my own.

"I need..."

"Fuck!" His mouth came down on mine again. This time, there was hunger and need the first kiss had only hinted at. It threatened to devour me. I couldn't think. Couldn't do anything but feel. Warlock's hard body pressed against mine, his arms holding me to him tightly. *It all felt so fucking good!* "Sweet as honey."

I wound my arms around his neck, holding on for dear life as the kiss went on and on. The longer he kept it up, the more under his spell I fell. My whimpers filled the air. Every sound I made seemed to encourage Warlock. Or maybe it confirmed to him he had me pegged. The man could control me with his kiss alone.

That wasn't the problem, though. The problem was, I didn't care if he controlled me, as long as he didn't stop his sinful, wicked mouth.

Chapter Five
Warlock

I've had more women than I care to admit. I was faithful to Bev, but before that, I'd indulged often. Never had any woman affected me the way Hope did. She made something inside me click into place. Holding her in my arms had felt right from the very first time. Now, I knew there was no way I ever wanted to be without her. I needed the right to hold her tightly against me. She was innocence and light, a goodness I didn't deserve but couldn't give up. She was the other half of my tattered soul. I knew it beyond a doubt.

But how could I keep her? Was it even right to try?

She soaked up my affection like a sponge, eager for my touch. I had no clue if it was me she wanted or if any man who was kind to her and gave her the physical tenderness she craved would do for her. She hadn't responded to any of the advances the guys in the club had thrown her way -- and there were many. Razor wasn't the only one. He'd said that, if I gave her what she needed, she'd be loyal to me. True. Not like Bev. But did I believe him? That was the fucking question. At this moment, I thought I might. I wanted to believe him because I wanted this woman to be mine. She might be a little broken, but so was I. Maybe my mother was right. Maybe Hope was the one woman in the world who could be what I needed.

I lifted her, urging her legs around my waist. Unlike at the beach, she obeyed eagerly, locking her ankles. I walked us to the bed, not sure if I was going to actually make her mine or not. We hadn't talked about this, and now wasn't the time. I wasn't sure I had it in me to stop unless she put the brakes on. Judging by the way she'd started responding to my kiss -- and making her own demands -- I doubted she'd be the one stopping this.

"Fuck... fuck!" I chanted the mantra as I tried to keep a rein on myself. Mainly because Hope had figured out how to move on me to get the friction on her clit she needed. In the process, she was driving me fucking crazy.

"I -- Oh, my God! Oh, God!" Hope trembled in my arms. Her body erupted in sweat, and her breath came quickly. I kissed her again, wanting to catch her cries. Not because I didn't want her to make noise. Those sounds were mine. I was greedy for them.

She tensed, then she trembled, gripping my shoulders spasmodically. Her thighs tightened around my hips, and she screamed as she came, her eyes wide and looking straight into mine.

When she relaxed, Hope gazed up at me in wonder. I knew then that was her first orgasm. She didn't say anything, stared at me, her face slowly flushing a deep scarlet. Tears sprang to her eyes, and she darted her gaze away from mine. Immediately, I caught her chin in my hand, forcing her to look up at me. For long moments I said nothing, stared into her eyes. I was so fucking hard I was about to come in my shorts, but now wasn't the time. Not until after we'd talked about it. And I could see by the startled expression on her face, Hope wasn't nearly ready for this. She wanted it, but she wasn't ready.

"You OK, honey?"

"Did I do something wrong?" Her voice was barely above a whisper.

"No, baby. You did everything right. We need to talk, but not right now." I rolled over, taking her with me. Pulling Hope solidly against my chest, I settled her so that she was draped half over me with her head on my shoulder. My arms were around her tightly -- I'd never held a woman so tightly! This was so surreal. It wasn't something I'd ever have done if the damned woman hadn't bewitched me or something. I didn't want another woman in my life. Not after Bev. Because I knew I'd never trust anyone with what little heart I had ever again.

"I *did* do something wrong. You stopped. I thought -- I mean -- You didn't…"

"I know, baby. We haven't talked about this, and I never meant to kiss you, let alone get this far."

"Oh." Her body was stiff, and I knew she was going to bolt. Or at least she was going to try.

"Yeah." I heaved in a breath. I was going to have to let her go, but my arms wouldn't relax. I found myself muttering, "Now that I've had a taste, ain't sure I can survive without another."

"What?" She sounded so confused I wanted to kick myself.

"Stay here with me a while, Hope. Relax. We'll talk later and figure out what to do next."

She did as I instructed. Lay in my arms until she dozed off. It was late afternoon, and she'd had a full day. We were both still in our swimming clothes, though they'd pretty much dried. She'd be uncomfortable, but I didn't want her to wake with me groping her while I undressed her. This had gone way too far. Way too fucking far.

I waited about fifteen minutes. When she didn't move and her breathing remained deep and even, I slipped out from underneath her, tucking a blanket around her. I knew I was damned. No way could I keep my distance from her. Not after this. She was like the most addictive drug. Once I'd had a taste, I needed more. It was only a matter of time before I fucked her into oblivion. Once that happened, there was no way in hell I'd ever let her go.

* * *

Hope

The next two weeks were the most confusing of my life. Warlock stayed away from me during the day but couldn't seem to get enough of me at night. At least, he'd given me more orgasms than I could count. He never penetrated me, and he never actually touched me or even got me naked. It was the same scene over and over again. I wanted more but didn't know how to ask for it. I also wasn't certain he wanted anything more. I was more than ignorant about sex, but I knew this couldn't be normal.

Maybe it was his age or something? I mean, he was hard all the time. Every time he came to me, I could see the bulge in his jeans. He didn't try to hide it, and I heard several of the men in the club laughing at him and commenting on it. No one ever made a crude comment about me, but they seemed to take delight in his discomfort. Which was when it hit me. I might not know much about sex or sexual relationships, but I knew enough to know that men didn't walk around in that state. They took care of it. Which meant, if he wasn't getting it from me, he was most likely getting it from someone else.

"You look like you have the weight of the world on your shoulders, Hope." Esther came up beside me where I was decorating salt-dough ornaments with a small group of young children. She put her arm around my shoulders and squeezed once. "What's wrong?"

"What? Oh! Nothing." I smiled brightly. "Just concentrating on my ornament."

"Really." The woman raised an eyebrow, then took the brush from my hand. "Might want to concentrate on something else, then."

I looked down and gasped. The back of my left hand was covered in green paint and gold glitter. The children giggled. I frowned at the little monsters. "Why didn't you guys say something? I thought we were besties!"

One little girl about nine, Jerrica, grinned at me. "We were watching. You been doing it since that guy Warlock left. You always go all spacey whenever he's around." They all giggled again.

"Thanks, guys. Way to have a girl's back." I wasn't really upset with them, but they seemed to enjoy picking on me. It was all in good fun, and they always, *always*, hugged me afterward. I think I enjoyed the hugs more than they did.

"He looks like Santa." Jerrica glanced wistfully at the door Warlock had disappeared through about ten minutes ago. My heart ached for the child. She reminded me too much of myself. While the nuns allowed some secular things, like Santa, around us at Christmas, it was never a big production or anything for us to get attached to. Christmas was about the birth of Jesus and the hope He represented for humanity. Which I embraced with all my heart. As I'd gotten older and saw the impact of a jolly old Elf giving gifts to other kids, I always felt I'd missed out on something magical. Not so much for the toys or presents or whatever, but the lesson in it. Christmas is a time of giving. Which was why this whole Christmas party thing was becoming so important to me. This bunch of badass bikers was doing something important for the community. Each child here was experiencing something they'd never forget as well as learning an important life lesson.

"He does, doesn't he?" I reached out to Jerrica with my green hand, and the girl backed away from me.

"Oh, no. Wash your hands first. Green is not my color." Everyone around me laughed, including myself.

"No, but gold glitter certainly is." I lunged for Jerrica, pretending I was going to cover her in the paint from my hand. This brought on more laughter before Jerrica threw herself into my arms, laughing so hard she shook with it.

"I love you, Hope! You can get green paint on me if you want to."

I hugged the girl back, recognizing the longing in her for what it was. She was as lonely as I had been at her age. Still was. Especially since Mrs. Wagner had passed away.

"I love you too, Jerrica." My heart ached for the girl. I wanted so much to bring her into my life, but there was no way I was in any shape to adopt any child. Or even have my own. I was only here temporarily before I had to go back to Indiana. To see my marriage annulled.

I held her until she pulled back. She smiled at me, but I could see the sheen of tears in her eyes. I was sure she saw them in mine as well.

Getting up from my seat, I went to the bathroom to wash my hands. Took some doing, but I finally got most of the paint off. As I looked in the mirror, I could see so many changes in myself. Physical as well as emotional.

I looked happier than I had for a long while.

Even though my skin seemed to stay on the verge of being burnt, I had a healthy glow that had never been there before. There were equal parts pain and happiness in my eyes. The juxtaposition seemed both cruel and obscene. I was only going to be happy as long as I was here. In the Black Reign compound. With Warlock. All that was going away sooner rather than later. I was hoping they'd let me stay until after Christmas. Being alone for Christmas seemed like the most intolerable thing in the world right now.

I was finishing up when the door opened. I'd seen the woman around the clubhouse at parties. While I'd never spoken with her, I'd seen her giving me superior smirks every time she saw me.

"Hope, isn't it?" The woman was tall and curvy. Large breasts were encased perfectly in the leather vest she wore. Cleavage galore. Tight leather pants with laces from her ankle to the waistband hugged her slender legs and luscious hips like a second skin. The material must have had more give to it than it looked because, otherwise, they were so tight there was no way she could even sit in them. On her feet were six-inch platform pumps. How could the woman walk? But she did. Routinely. I'd seen her. The men seemed to love it.

"Yes. I've seen you around." It was stupid, but I didn't know what else to say.

She gave me that same smirk as she looked down at me from her dominant height. "I hear you're getting ready to go back to Indiana." She turned from me then, pulling out a tube of blood-red lipstick from between her breasts and opening it to apply to her already-coated lips.

"At some point, yes."

"Pretty soon from what I hear. Wrath did some

magic and got things moving. I suspect you'll be leaving in a day or two."

"Oh." *Stupid*! I couldn't seem to form words around this woman. She was perfect. Every hair in place. Make-up done to perfection. Perfect body. Confident. Intelligent. She was a woman who screamed sex. Probably everything Warlock expected in a woman. Everything I wasn't.

"Don't worry. I'll make sure Warlock is taken care of." She gave a low, husky laugh. "Like I've been doing since he got here."

I felt sick. Was this where Warlock had been going at night after I fell asleep? After he'd spent time coaxing me to an orgasm? Did he find me that lacking in sexual knowledge? What was I thinking? Of course, he found me lacking! I was a virgin in both thought and deed. I'd spent my teenage years in a nursing home. My younger years in a Catholic group home. The things I'd done with Warlock had all been firsts for me. While I'd loved every second of it, had he been frustrated with me? Or worse, laughing at me?

Trying for a smile when I really wanted to throw up, I nodded like an idiot. "That's good, then. I wouldn't want him to be alone." Then I pushed past her and left the bathroom.

Instead of going back to the common room with the children and the Black Reign women, I went to my room to get myself under control. This had to stop. As much as I wanted Warlock, as much as I wanted to do right by Mrs. Wagner, I had to think about myself in this instance. If I wanted any self-respect, I had to get out of here. I thought Mrs. Wagner would understand because she always told me women were not doormats for their men to push them around. They stood up for themselves and demanded as much respect from their men as they gave back. Anything less was doing everyone a disservice.

It was time to leave.

I didn't want to take too many of the things the women had gotten for me. I needed underwear and a couple pairs of jeans and shorts, as well as three or four T-shirts. I picked out the best, most comfortable pair of shoes and three pairs of socks and stuffed everything in my backpack. It didn't feel right taking off without at least finding Esther and thanking her and the other women. I dreaded it, though. I knew it would hurt the other woman's feelings, and she'd likely do her best to get me to stay, but I couldn't. I had written all their numbers down from the phone they'd given me, though I hadn't taken the phone. I'd find a way to call them after I got back to Indiana. Then I'd send money to pay for the clothing I'd taken with me.

Swiping a tear from my cheek, I headed down the stairs and outside the main building. I'd taken the back way so I didn't run into any of the women or the children. That was when I remembered Jerrica. I couldn't leave that little girl without saying goodbye. It would break her heart. Might anyway.

This was going to suck.

* * *

Warlock

"You're gonna have to make a fuckin' decision, brother." Wrath had hunted me down, pulling me into his office for a come-to-Jesus meeting. "I'm ready to move on getting your marriage annulled, but I have to have your signature. You won't answer Shotgun, you won't return the affidavit I gave you with your signature. I need to know what you want to do. Wasted enough fuckin' time on this if you're not participating."

"I'll sign the thing when I'm Goddamned good and ready."

"You better get good and ready," he snapped. "Or get your ass to figuring out how you're gonna keep that girl."

I narrowed my eyes. "That sounds suspiciously close to a threat. You've got a woman. You throwin' her over?"

"Hell, no! Celeste is my whole entire world. As are Holly and Tabitha. Those girls are everything I could have ever wanted in my life, and I'll guard them with my life."

"Then what are you hinting at, Wrath?"

"More than one brother here has eyes on her. The only reason they haven't moved yet is because they're waiting for you to decide what you want to do. It's more of a courtesy than they'd normally offer, but they've had the fear of El Diablo put into them. He's built you up. How you're such a badass and can help this club in ways most of them can't conceive of." He scowled at me. "We all know how you sacrificed your woman for your club. While El Diablo said you had little choice, most of us think you'll chew Hope up and spit her out."

"I'm aware of how fragile she is. More so than you."

"You think?" Wrath tilted his head slightly. Obviously the man knew more than I thought. "Shotgun and Esther came through in spades. They dug up everything about that girl there was to know. They probably know more about her background than she does." He scowled at me. "And you're leading her on. Everyone knows you spend most of the night with her, yet you leave before she wakes. Anyone can see how that's messing with her head. You're hurting her, Warlock." Wrath pointed a finger at me in a stabbing motion. "Make up your fuckin' mind."

"Fuck." I scrubbed my hand over my face. "I don't know what to fuckin' do."

"It's not that hard, man. Either you take a chance on her or you don't. She's all in, brother. Anyone can see that."

"Yeah, but she's not in it for the right reasons."

"How do you know? What makes you think that? She said she hates you or that she wants someone else?"

"Wrath, it's not that simple. She's nineteen years old with no real-world experience. I'm forty-nine. Thirty years I've got on her. She's with me because she sees me as something stable in her life. What happens in five years when she realizes she's shackled to an old man instead of someone closer to her age? She's not gonna grow old with me. She's gonna watch me age and die way before she does."

"God. I never pegged you for such a pussy, Warlock." Wrath chuckled as he shook his head. "Or a stupid-ass motherfucker."

"I'm leaving." I stood. I wasn't sitting here and taking this from Wrath. "This is my life. Not yours."

"Sit your ass down." The disapproving growl came from behind me. I looked to see Samson, the vice president of Black Reign, enter and slam the door behind him. He looked livid. With a long-suffering sigh, I did as I was told. If I'd been in Samson's position, I'd have busted my ass for the disrespect. Samson looked like he wanted to do that. "This is the only time we're having this discussion, and I'm only doing it because Lottie made me." That got a raised eyebrow from me. Which must have been more than the big man could take. Instantly, his fist shot out and connected with my jaw. "You ain't president here, Warlock. Way you're goin', you ain't gonna be here much longer. While you are here, though, you will show proper respect to the officers in this club." Surprisingly, Samson didn't look or sound all that angry. Well, he didn't look or sound any angrier than he usually did. His default setting seemed to be surly-ass motherfucker. The only time I'd ever seen a different expression on his face was when his woman, Charlotte -- Lottie -- was with him.

I gritted my teeth and closed my eyes, taking a much-needed deep breath. "Noted."

Samson sat down on the other end of the couch from me. I honestly didn't blame the guy. It was hard to take when I was used to being the one doing the punishing. "Lottie sees how much Hope is struggling. Especially the last couple of weeks. Funny how the timing puts that about the same time you started sleeping with her." He gave me a hard look. "If you're fuckin' her and ain't committed to her, I'm gonna have to tell you to make a decision. Right now. Either you're keepin' her, or Wrath is pushing through this annulment in record fuckin' time. Got more than one brother here wanting to take her in, Warlock. She'll make someone a fine ol' lady. If she doesn't get scared off."

"Or beaten down," Wrath added. "You're pushing toward the second more than the first."

"I've not fucked her... just fooled around a bit. And I've *never* indicated to her she was less than me. Not once."

"Yes, you have." Samson stretched out his long legs, tensing his arm muscles so the veins stood out in a show of his raw power. I was big and strong. Samson was on a whole other level. "Every single night when you leave her." I knew he was right. "She's got her shit packed, Warlock. Trying to leave even now. Esther is making her say goodbye to everyone before she leaves, which bought us a few minutes to confront you."

"Leaving?" That got my back up. "What the fuck do you mean, leaving? We agreed she'd stay here until we resolved the marriage issue."

"Yeah? Well, seems you blew it, buddy. 'Cause she's definitely leaving. If she hadn't felt guilty about leaving without saying goodbye, especially to Esther and that little girl who's taken up with her, she'd be long gone."

"Who's givin' her a ride? I'll kill the motherfucker!" My temper was spiking, despite the warning Samson had given me earlier.

"Watch it..." Samson growled.

I stood, pacing across the office. Wrath sat with his feet on the desk, his hands behind his head. Samson looked ready to pounce. My jaw was still sore where the man had punched me, reminding me he meant business.

"She's got nowhere to go. You can't let her leave."

"Oh, we don't intend to." Wrath grinned when my gaze snapped to him.

"Nope. Like I said. Got more than one brother ready to take her on. You give us the word, and Wrath will fix this annulment thing. Razor has first dibs. She won't take him, Jekyll's next. She don't want him, Loki believes he can get her to agree to be his." Samson gave me a level look that said he was dead serious.

"Loki." I put a disgusted sneer in my voice. "He's as old as me. He's got no business getting near Hope."

"That's where your thinking is flawed, Warlock." Samson stood in a fluid, quick movement, striding the three steps to stand nose to nose with me. "She don't care about age. Jax? Mars? She's polite to them, but she ignores their advances. Isn't comfortable with them. The whole compound noticed it. Givin' Jax hell about it, too. Mars shrugs it off, saying he knew the second he saw her she wouldn't have a man who wasn't in his prime. She's lived through too much to be with a man who still has growing to do. I suspect you know that. If not, you didn't talk to her nearly enough before you started a physical relationship with her."

"I did. She said she didn't want a guy her age." I turned to look out the window. I needed to think, but it didn't look like I had that kind of time.

"I've told El Diablo from the very beginning you were fucking stupid." Wrath moved his feet off his desk and took out a piece of paper from his desk drawer. "Sign the fuckin' paper, Warlock." His gaze was deadly. "That girl ain't goin' nowhere, and you ain't brave enough to take her on. We'll take it from here. If you are? You do it now. You take her, and you show her she's worthy of the man hand-picked by El Diablo to be the fucking enforcer of this club."

No pressure there.

Chapter Six
Hope

"I've really got to go." I could feel the net closing around me. Esther and Celeste had started a campaign to have me see every single person in this clubhouse. Or so it seemed. The last person they took me to was Jerrica.

"Please don't leave, Hope." Jerrica looked up at me with big brown eyes, and I felt the tears gather in my eyes. "Stay with me."

"I can't, sweetie," I said, pulling the little girl into my arms. "I don't live here. I was visiting."

"You *should* live here," Celeste muttered, throwing a glance over my shoulder. Immediately, I turned. Wrath, Celeste's husband, entered the room with a lazy stroll. With him, Razor and Jekyll made their way to our little group. Both Jekyll and Razor had been kind to me, helping me with the popcorn stringing and organizing the kids to make salt-dough ornaments. I'd been incredibly comfortable with both of them, but they felt more like brothers or trusted friends than anything else. I had to face it -- my heart had seized on Warlock. And he wasn't attainable.

"What's going on?" I stood. Jerrica retained hold of my hand.

"Sweet Hope." El Diablo and Jezebel entered from the other side of the room. I felt like I was being surrounded. "We want you to stay. If you're uncomfortable here, you need only say so, and I'll make it better."

"No. Everyone's been incredibly nice." I looked away, remembering the woman from the restroom. Of course, El Diablo didn't miss much. Neither did Jezebel.

"If the club girls are harassing you…" Jezebel began, but El Diablo put his hand on her shoulder, and she stilled.

"It's time I left. This was a fantasy when it started. Now, it's pitiful." There. I'd admitted it out loud. I took a deep breath. "You've all been so good to me. I can't thank you enough."

"At least stay through Christmas." Esther took my other hand, bringing it to her cheek to rub against her skin like a cat might. As if she really cared about me. There were tears in her eyes, and she seemed to be silently pleading with me to do as she asked. "You're my friend. I'm not ready for you to leave."

"I can't stay, Esther. I --" Tears threatened, and my throat closed up.

"You know," Razor spoke as he approached me. "There're more men here than Warlock. He's an ass on the best of days, honey. More than one of us is willing to make a try for you." He shook his head. "And I ain't just talkin' about a physical relationship. You'd make a good, strong ol' lady. Give me a chance, and I'll prove I can make you happy."

I sucked in a breath. "Razor? Why would you do that?"

"I don't know what bullshit Warlock's been feedin' you, but you're worth takin' a chance on. His loss is my gain."

"Oh, Razor." I launched myself into his arms. "You're such a good person. I knew it from the day I met you. You were so gentle and patient with me." I let him go, but he kept his arms around me when I pulled back. "You know I can't do this. Much as I love it here, much as I love you, it's not like that."

He grinned. "Bet I could change your mind."

I couldn't help it. I laughed even as tears

overflowed. "You're crazy."

"Ain't denyin' that, but I'll say this. Any man who doesn't want to make you his own is a fuckin' fool."

"You don't want Razor, what about me?" Jekyll moved in beside me, taking me from Razor's arms and pulling me into his.

"I can't believe you guys." Maybe I'd underestimated the friends I'd made here. "I thought everyone was only nice to me because of Warlock."

"Honey, why in the world would you think that?" Jekyll frowned down at me but didn't let me go.

"Because I don't belong here."

"Again," Jekyll said, his frown deepening, "why would you think that?"

"If anything, we all like you *despite* Warlock." Razor buried his hand in my hair, massaging my scalp affectionately. "He's the asshole to make assholes ashamed of being assholes."

"There are many more in line, Hope." El Diablo put his arm around Jezebel and kissed her temple as he spoke. "You need a strong protector. A family of your own. I hope you'll grow to think of all of us as a family, but I want you to have the one thing you've never had for yourself."

The tears did come then. Steady streams of the vile things. Jekyll pulled me close, his strong arms comforting. But it didn't feel right. I knew I was safe, and that he'd give me whatever emotional support I needed, but he wasn't what I wanted. Or needed.

"I appreciate all you're trying to do, but --"

"Get your motherfucking hands off her, Jekyll!"

Warlock. He stormed into the common room looking positively enraged. My heart leapt. I wasn't frightened. Not of Warlock. Looking at him now, coming for me, was like looking at my dreams all coming true. A miracle. I had no idea why he was here or why he was angry, only that my heart wanted him to be coming for me.

"Well, I guess that answers that question." Razor moved in front of Warlock, preventing him from reaching me. I struggled to get free from Jekyll, but he leaned down to whisper in my ear.

"Be still a while longer, honey. I promise you it will be worth it."

I looked up at him. He winked at me "I know you love him. Don't pretend to know why, but everyone in this whole place sees it."

"Am I a fool?" I wasn't sure I could take it if he said I was.

"Not at all, honey. He's the fool for not being man enough to give you what you want. My advice?" I nodded at him. "Make the asshole work for it. Show him more of what you gave him the first day you met him."

I ducked my head. "Despite what it looked like that day, I'm not a violent person."

"You were taking him to task for not respecting you and the memory of a woman you loved." Jekyll leaned down and kissed my forehead. When Warlock erupted behind me, I knew that kiss was for show. The man winked at me. "That makes you worth fighting for, Hope. Any woman who'd attack a man more than twice her size for those she loves is worth everything."

The next thing I knew, I was snatched away from Jekyll and into Warlock's arms. I wanted nothing more than to wrap my arms around him and cling to him so tightly I'd never be separated from him again. But there were too many issues separating us. The woman in the bathroom, for one thing.

I struggled, trying to get away from him when it was the last thing I wanted. I'd fought too hard for my self-respect to fall into his arms, no matter how much I wanted it. There had to be some reasonable expectations set for both of us.

"Let me go, Warlock."

"I'm pretty sure I told you to fuckin' call me Max." His growl was as sexy as it was arrogant.

"At this point, I could give two shits what you want." I tried to keep my voice calm, recognizing that I needed to keep my cool. Until I couldn't. I glanced at Jekyll, which seemed to set Warlock off.

"Don't look at him! You're my woman. Not his!"

"I'm not yours either. You've made that abundantly clear. As of this moment, I'm done with anyone choosing who I let into my life. Not your mother. Not you. No one. I'll choose for myself."

"You already chose." Warlock tightened his grip on me. Until I hiked my knee into his groin.

"Mother fuck!" He dropped me immediately and bent at the waist. I backed up several steps before confronting him.

"When I tell you to let me go, I mean it. You told me once I had to accept the consequences of my actions. These are yours."

More than one of the men in the room laughed. Razor outright guffawed. Warlock tried to glare at the man, but there was still a grimace of pain on his face so he couldn't pull it off very well.

"Now we're getting somewhere." That came from El Diablo, who'd sat in a comfortable-looking chair and pulled his wife into his lap. He snapped his fingers, and the man behind the bar poured him a glass of Woodford Reserve and brought it to him. Jezebel promptly took it from her husband and downed it, handing it back to the prospect. The man chuckled.

"What'd you do that for? You know I'm not gonna hurt you." Warlock sounded genuinely perplexed. "I thought you liked what we do in private?"

"I do. But there are boundaries. Especially since I found out where you've been going at night after you leave me." I couldn't help the hurt in my voice. "How could you?"

He blinked, jerking back like I'd struck him again. "Honey, I've been going back to my room. Or sitting outside your door until daylight. Where did you think I've been goin'?"

"Don't lie!" I shouted the command. "Do not lie to me, Maximilian. I know about the woman you've been going to."

"What?" El Diablo barked. "Warlock!"

"I swear I have no idea what you're talking about, Hope. I've only been with two women in the last seven years. Bev, my ol' lady. And you."

"You've not really been with me, though. Have you?" I looked him directly in the eyes. I needed to see the truth of it there. I couldn't really tell if he was lying so much as I could tell when he was holding back from me. He'd been doing a lot of that lately.

He closed his eyes, obviously trying to get himself under control. "Come with me, Hope. We'll talk this out and see where we go from here."

"You said that last time," I snapped. "Sure, I've been getting some pretty good orgasms out of the deal, but that's all I've been getting! You've got one foot out the door! You don't want me, but you don't want anyone else to have me either!" Voicing the facts as I saw them made it abundantly clear I *had* been playing the fool. "I've been playing the part of lovesick teenager. Letting you do whatever you wanted and hoping you'd decide I was what you wanted. Or, at least, that you'd give me a chance to be what you needed. But you know what? It's not fucking worth it!" I rarely ever swore, but if there was ever a time for it, it was now. "Fuck you, Warlock. I'm done."

"That's my girl." Jekyll spoke softly from behind me, his hand going to my shoulder. I nearly broke down into tears. Grief and frustration were strong inside me. I felt like I was losing Mrs. Wagner all over again. Was she disappointed in me for not being able to be what her son needed?

I turned to go, but, to my surprise, Esther, Celeste, and Noell surrounded me, putting their arms around me. I was effectively cut off from any of the men, though Jekyll had his arms around Celeste and Esther while Razor was on the other side, his hands on the shoulders of Celeste and Noelle.

"Well," El Diablo's smooth voice filled the void after I'd told Warlock off. "I guess that's that. Warlock, I think that tells me all I needed to know."

"I'm not leaving her, El Diablo. She's mine, legally. And I'm not giving her up."

"Wrath can take care of the legality of that tie. In fact, did you not sign the affidavit he prepared? The one declaring you a victim of fraud?"

"He didn't." Samson strolled into the room, Wrath right behind him.

"I'm not giving her up."

"Yeah?" Once I'd started this, I couldn't seem to help myself. The frustration that had been building for the weeks I'd been here finally boiling over. "Well, maybe I'm giving you up! Ever think of that? You can have your stupid club girls, or whatever they're called. I don't care anymore!" I practically screamed the last.

Unfortunately, the tears streaming down my face belied the statement I didn't care. "You're an asshole, Warlock. A complete and utter asshole!"

"Seems like the girl doesn't want to go with you." Razor looked over his shoulder, not removing his embrace from the other women. It wasn't so much that he was hugging them, but like all of them were hugging *me*. The men cemented the hold the women had on me so no one could break it.

Warlock scrubbed a hand over his face. "Five minutes, Hope. Give me five minutes alone with you."

"You don't have to, Hope." Jekyll shook his head. "Not if you don't want to."

I thought about it a minute, staring hard at Warlock. His expression was blank, but he held his breath. I could almost see Mrs. Wagner smiling at me encouragingly, telling me to "Go on, dear girl. Listen to what he has to say."

"Fine." I gently moved out of the arms of the woman and past Razor, who was between me and Warlock. "Five minutes. That's it. And only because I loved your mother, Warlock. I don't know what you're playing at now, but this is it. After this, I'm done."

He nodded once, then reached his hand out to me. Instead of taking it, I gave him a withering look and lifted my chin, walking past him in a huff. Halfway up the stairs, he caught me, snagging my hand anyway.

"Not a word until we get inside my room," he growled.

"I have nothing to say to you." I didn't look at him, keeping my eyes straight ahead. As if that could diminish his presence. He was larger than life. Ignoring him was an impossibility. I tried, though.

"Then you'll listen to me."

We reached his room, and he shoved the door open, dragging me in after him. The second he'd slammed the door shut, he wrapped his arms around my waist and lifted. Automatically, my legs went around his hips as he mashed me between the door and his hard body.

"You're not leaving me, Hope." Warlock had buried his face against my neck. His growled words sent butterflies surging through my stomach, and I shivered. "You're my wife. I'm makin' you my woman. Right now."

"No!" I said weakly, clinging to him rather than pushing him away. "That woman said she'd been taking care of you since you got here. I'm not that pathetic!"

"I have no idea what woman you're talking about, and I don't care. I'm telling you the truth when I say you're the only woman I've been with. We might not have fucked yet, but I haven't even looked at a woman since I met you, Hope."

I wanted to believe him. I really did. "How am I supposed to believe that, Max? You can't seem to decide if you like me or if I'm a nuisance. A man as skilled as you are at pleasuring a woman doesn't go without female companionship long. Apparently, I'm not very good at whatever it is you like."

"Stop, Hope! I was trying my damnedest to do the right thing by you!"

"How is giving me so much pleasure and holding me until I sleep, then leaving me doing right?" I wanted to slap his too-handsome face. "Let me down!"

Instead of doing what I asked, he carried me to the bed and set me down beside it. Then, to my surprise, he whipped off his shirt. He snagged both my hands, forcing them open with his thumbs, placing them flat on his chest.

"This is yours, Hope. All of me."

"I ain't sharing, Max." I yanked my hands away. "I don't even know if I want you or not. You've hurt me worse than anyone in my life ever has! Damn you!"

I shoved him then. Hard. He didn't move. So I did it again. And again. I screamed at him and shoved one more time. The next thing I knew I was in his arms. I'd pulled off my own shirt and shrugged out of my bra so that I was against him skin to skin. My mouth found his, and I kissed him for all I was worth.

Warlock's big hands were at my waist, unfastening my shorts and shoving them along with my panties down my hips to pool at my feet. Somehow, he had his pants down to his knees, his cock standing proud between us. I felt the tip poking my entrance. Suddenly it was the most important thing in my world to get it inside me.

I hopped up so I could wrap my legs around his waist and shifted until I felt myself sinking down around his thickness. It stretched and burned until I reached a point where I couldn't go any farther without pain.

"Now what'er you gonna do, girl?" His growl was more of a challenge than him mocking me for getting in a situation I wasn't ready for.

"I hate you!" I yelled at him. Then I forced myself fully down on him with a wild scream. I felt like I'd ripped in two. The pain was intense. I wanted off him, but I was afraid to move.

"I know, honey. I know. And you have every right to hate me. I've not treated you like I should have." He had his arm clamped around me tightly as he moved us to the bed, him on top of me. "Look at me, Hope. My beautiful, sweet Hope." He brushed his other hand over my hair, moving strands off my forehead. I obeyed him more on instinct than out of any wish to comply with the arrogant pig. "I'm sorry. I'm sorry for everything, but most especially for not talking to you like I demanded you do to me."

"You're a shithead." I sniffed. It was a combination of pain, frustration, and sadness. "I didn't want to lose you. I know I never really had you to begin with, but I don't want to *not* have you at all! At least until now, I got to be with you. But I can't keep looking like an idiot. I'm taking what I want from you right now. After this is over, after I have this one experience with you to treasure for the rest of my life, I'm outta here, Max. You can do whatever you want to with the annulment."

He shook his head, moving out of me slightly only to ease back in. Farther this time. It burned and stretched, and I cried out. I wasn't sure if it was pain or that glorious pleasure I knew I'd always find in his arms.

"You're not leaving me, Hope. Not now that I finally have some hope in my life." He did that slow glide in and out of me again. There was less pain and more pleasure. There was still a burn, but the sharp pinch was gone. "You gave that to me. Hope. You're aptly named."

"Why now?" I had to know. "If this is you needing to get your fill, don't bother with the pretty words. I'm serious. This is it. What we share in the next few minutes will have to do us both."

He moved again. Watching me carefully, he slid out. Then back inside. "I knew the first moment I laid eyes on you you'd be mine, Hope. I didn't want to admit it. Not even to myself. But when you declared

Maximilian Wagner was your man, my very first thought was, 'Yes, I am.' I told you about Bev. I told you what happened."

"She betrayed you and your club, so you killed her."

"Yes. I remember you asking me if that was a warning to you."

"You said it was."

He shook his head. "I lied, Hope. I could never harm you or let anyone else harm you."

The pressure between my legs where we were joined eased until even the dull ache was gone. In its place, my clit throbbed with my heartbeat, and pleasure started to build. It was slow in coming, but persistent. Distracting. This conversation was too important for me to not give it my full attention, but I couldn't. I knew it was only a matter of time before my mind shut down altogether. This was nothing like what we'd done before. Though Warlock had touched my body, had given me more pleasure than I'd ever thought possible, this promised to eclipse the past.

"You did before. What makes you think I'm any different?"

"Because, even though I loved Bev, she never truly entrenched herself in my heart. I knew from the outset she wasn't the woman for me. I wanted to believe her lies because I think I missed that closeness a man can only have with his family. I wanted that so much, I compromised myself."

"And your club?"

He nodded. "And my club." Again, he slid out of me, then back in. He watched me carefully, never taking his eyes from me. Not letting me look away from him. "The thing is, Bev didn't care. She had a goal, and it had nothing to do with me. You said from the very beginning you wanted to be the woman I needed. You wanted to make me happy. And you've done everything you can to accomplish that. You've done everything I've asked you to. You didn't question me, even when I hurt you. You should have, Hope. No one, not even me, gets to hurt you like I did and not answer for it."

"You're confusing me! I can't think like this!" I was becoming more than a little desperate. My hips bucked to his, my body needing more than he was giving. I needed him to move faster. "Oh, my God, Max! What's happening to me?"

I gasped in a breath as he shifted his position a fraction, putting more friction on my clit. As I looked up into his eyes, he seemed so calm. So centered when I was a chaotic, emotional mess. When he stroked inside me this time, shockwaves shot through me in an explosive storm. I screamed before I realized I was going to scream. My fingers gripped his biceps, digging in as deep as I could to hold on to him. The need to anchor myself was an instinct I couldn't deny. I felt like I was flying off into space, my body fragmenting into a million pieces.

"That's it, my beautiful Hope. Let it come. Let me have you."

"Please, Max! Oh, God! Please!" I had no idea what I was begging for. Good thing he seemed to. Warlock quickened his pace, thrusting with ever-increasing strokes. Sweat slickened his skin, and his features hardened as he rode me. Harder and harder he moved. There was no longer any pain. Only an almost unbearable pleasure that didn't seem to have an end.

"That's it, Hope. Come again for me. Come on my fuckin' cock!" His voice was husky, sexy. His body gliding against mine was the most erotic sensation. He seemed to be holding onto his control by a thread. I had no control.

When Warlock told me to come, I was helpless to do anything but obey him. My body seized, my muscles tightening to the point of pain. When my orgasm exploded through me once more, the edges of my vision began to darken, and pinpricks of light filled the blackening field. I could see nothing but Warlock's fierce expression, then the shock as my pussy clamped down around him. With his own war bellow to the ceiling, Warlock let himself go. He buried himself deep inside me, and I felt his seed fill me, hot and soothing. Something settled inside me. It was as if I'd waited my whole life for this moment. This man. For the first time in my life, I felt like all might not be well, but it could get there with some work. If he gave me the chance, I could prove to him we belonged together. This was where I wanted to be. With Warlock. With Maximilian Wagner. I was...

Home.

Chapter Seven
Warlock

Never in my life had I felt such peace than the moment when I emptied myself inside Hope. This was my woman. The one person in the whole world I knew could heal my battered soul. The worry I'd once had that she'd somehow betray me now seemed foolish. Hope wasn't that kind of woman. She wanted permanent personal attachments too much for that. When she made a friend, when she took a lover, she was all in. She'd be loyal, no matter what, because the relationship meant that much to her. Now, she was mine.

As I floated back down to earth, I realized I'd wrapped my arms around Hope tightly. I was also still on top of her, likely smothering or mashing her.

"Fuck." I loosened my grip and rolled us over. She whimpered and clung to me, keeping her hip over mine so my cock was still inside her. "You good? Did I hurt you?" She shook her head but didn't say anything. "Hope, look at me. Let me see your beautiful eyes." I brushed her cheek lightly with my thumb until she looked up at me. "There's my girl. Do you hurt? Do I need to put you in the bath to soak?" Again, she shook her head, tears leaking from the corner of her eyes. "I need words, Hope." I brushed away one tear gently with my fingertip. It had collected in the corner of her eye next to her nose, preparing to drip off the side.

"No." Her voice was barely above a whisper. She looked as shell-shocked as I felt. If I was going to convince her I was serious about us being together, about not dissolving our marriage, it was now or never.

"You sayin' that because it's the truth, or because you don't want to be alone?"

Finally, the dam burst. Hope's tears were my punishment. For everything. They'd hurt before, the first day I'd been such an ass when I found her with Razor playing with that fucking dog, but nothing like this. This whole situation, one I'd started, had been her goodbye. She'd wanted the sex I'd denied us both the previous weeks. Now that she'd gotten what she wanted, she was prepared to leave.

"Stop, baby. I can't take your tears -- they're killing me." She clung tightly. Like I was her lifeline. It felt better than I'd ever imagined even as her sorrow and grief gutted me like nothing else ever could. "I'm not going anywhere, Hope, and neither are you. We're married. There are bonds tying us together that can never be broken."

"You're d-doing exactly th-that! Wrath and Sh-Shotgun are f-fixing it! Y-you said s-so!"

"They were. Wrath gave me an ultimatum today. Sign the paper and let him file it, or claim you like we both want."

"But you h-hate me."

"Honey, do you think I'd come to you every single night if I hated you? Do my best to pleasure you?"

"You never st-stayed. If you liked me, you'd have stayed." She looked up at me then. There was so much sadness, so much longing, my heart broke. Right there. Looking into the clearest blue eyes I'd ever seen, my old, iron-clad heart shattered into a million pieces. "You didn't even want to have sex with me!"

"Baby, I wanted you so much I ached with it. I knew that once I had you, my choices would be taken away. As much as I thought I loved Bev, those feelings were nothing compared to what I feel for you. Believe it or not, it scared the living fuck outta me."

She met my gaze. "Are you going to leave now?"

"No, honey. My leaving you stops this second. I'm never leaving you again."

"Don't say that! You never wanted this! Not from the first second you saw that marriage certificate!"

"I did. I just didn't want to admit it." I pulled her tightly against me, positioning her so she lay on top of me. My cock was still firmly embedded inside her, my erection not diminishing even after coming my fucking brains out. "I'm going to admit something to you that I never thought I'd say. You know my mother and I had a contentious relationship at best. What you don't know, and what I never realized until the day you walked into my life, is that my mother knew her son. She knew what I needed even when I didn't. She always has. I thought this was all about you. That she wanted you safe and protected and loved when she knew you'd never had that in your life. At least not like I'd had it growing up. And it was. To a certain extent." I rubbed my hand up and down her back, hoping like hell it soothed her. "But it wasn't all about you. It was about me, too. She knew me well enough to know I needed you as much as you needed me. Even if we hadn't spoken in ten years. She knew."

She laid her head on my shoulder, her lips brushing softly against my neck. "I don't know what to believe."

"You give me this one last chance, and you'll know exactly what to believe, honey. One more chance. I'm telling you now I'm all in with this. With you." I squeezed her tightly. "With us."

"I want to. So much it hurts." She clung to me and shifted a bit. Probably getting comfortable. Then her breath caught.

"What is it, Hope? Do you hurt?"

"I -- no." She wiggled again and a whimper escaped her.

"Ahhh." I gave a shallow thrust inside her, my cock giving a very interested jerk. "I see."

"How can this feel so good?"

"You got me, baby. Sex has always been good, but I've never felt anything like what I feel when I'm inside you."

She raised her head to look down at me. Her delicate brows pinched together in confusion. "What do you mean? Doesn't it, you know, all feel the same?"

"I thought it did. Until I got my first taste of you. Hell, watching you come is an experience in itself. Makes me so fuckin' hard I nearly cream my pants every fuckin' time." I'd never talked dirty to her before. Now, I wanted to see how she'd react. Sure enough, her eyes got big, and her pussy clenched around me. She sucked in a startled breath and clutched my shoulders harder.

"Warlock?"

I thrust my hips upward, moving inside her in a slow, gentle glide. "Hurt?"

"What? No! There's no pain."

"Good." I urged her to sit, stopping my movement so she could adjust to the new sensations. "You're in control," I said. "Get a feel for what you like and how to move to get more of it."

"But... what if I do it wrong?"

"Baby, there's no right or wrong in this. You do what feels good. If you can't get there, you tell me, and I'll help you." I rested my hands on her thighs, rubbing up to her hips occasionally while she experimented with her movements.

She did exactly what I told her to do. Taking her time, she moved a few different ways, adjusting her position. Her body was tense, but I continued my slow stroking of her thighs and hips. Hope placed her hands on my chest, her arms framing her lovely breasts as she started a gentle rocking motion. Every now and then her pussy would spasm around me, and she'd shiver in reaction.

"Feel good?"

"Yes."

"How can I make it better?"

She shook her head, looking distressed. "I don't... I don't know!"

I moved my thumb to her clit and rubbed slightly. Instantly, her eyes got wide, and her mouth opened. Her pussy spasmed around me, and she shuddered once before her head fell back on her shoulders and she cried out. Her body erupted in sweat as she trembled around me. I pulled her back down so I could put my arms around her while she rode it out. Her hips moved in erratic snaps.

"That's it, baby. Fuck yourself like that." Again, her pussy gripped me and she groaned.

"You can't say things like that, Max!"

I grinned at her. "Why not? I think your little pussy likes it. I know my cock likes it when your pussy squeezes me."

She pushed up so she could look at me, her eyes wide. "You can feel that?"

"Oh, yeah. Which is why I'm gonna talk dirty to you every single time I get a chance." Hope bit her bottom lip and glanced away. "Tell me what you want. This only works if we talk to each other in everything."

"Will you... I mean, I like it when you're on top of me." Her breath caught as she spoke, and her skin was a lovely shade of pink. It should have looked odd with her reddish-orange hair, but she looked as beautiful as the day is long.

I pulled her down for a kiss and slowly rolled us so I was on top of her. Her legs tightened around my waist, and she met my kiss with kisses of her own. She was demanding without being aggressive, a trait unique to my Hope. There was no doubt in my mind now. Hope was the perfect woman for me. My mother knew me better than I knew myself, it seemed. I was sorry I would never be able to thank her.

* * *

Hope

The pleasure was overwhelming. Warlock was so far out of my league as to not even be believed. I didn't know how much I believed him when he said he wanted to be with me and knew I was a fool for initiating this, but I wanted the experience. I knew I'd never meet another man who made me feel things so intensely. He was larger than life. A man I'd built a fantasy around only to have it shattered. He hadn't been needlessly cruel to me like he had that first day, but it was painfully obvious he didn't really want me. Hearing him now, though…

Maybe I had one more chance in me. All I knew was, once Warlock was on top of me everything seemed to click into place. His kisses were intoxicating, making my head spin. I gripped his hips, digging my heels into his ass as he moved. Every stroke of his cock ignited a fire inside me I had no hope of smothering.

My breasts mashed against his chest, his chest hair abrading my nipples deliciously. There were so many new sensations I couldn't keep up. Warlock didn't seem to mind. He paid attention to my reactions and adjusted accordingly. His wicked encouragement was like another hand to pet me with, and I was as stimulated by his dirty words as I was by his cock deep inside me.

I came once more, my body seizing for several seconds before I was even able to scream. "Oh, God!"

"You ready for me to fuck you hard now?" Warlock's whisper in my ear was a wicked enticement. And sent me spiraling over the edge once again.

"Yes," I gasped. "Please, yes!"

I had no idea what I was asking for. When Warlock began surging into me with faster and harder strokes, I nearly lost my mind.

I thrashed and clawed at Warlock's back where I had my arms around him. I arched up to meet his hips so that our skin slapped loudly in the room. His grunts were as sexy as his words. I loved knowing he was taking pleasure in what he was doing. He'd yet to pull his cock out of me, even after he'd come the first time. Which was when it hit me.

"Warlock?" I tried to push him back, needing to say something.

"What is it, baby?" He continued to kiss me while he fucked me, though he'd slowed the pace somewhat.

"Mmmm…" God, I loved kissing him! He'd been my first kiss. The first guy to touch me. Given me my first orgasm… My brain was short circuiting!

"Tell me, baby. I can't make you feel good if you don't tell me what you need."

"You came inside me," I whispered.

"Believe me, I know, honey. And I never want to come anywhere else but in your sweet pussy." Then he grinned at me. "Unless it's in your sweet ass. Or your sweet mouth."

I was done.

I came in a wet rush, all the outrageous things he kept saying taking me over. The second I screamed, Warlock caught it with his mouth on mine, sweeping his tongue inside to tangle with mine. His movements sped up, as did the intensity. He growled as he kissed me, surging inside me in a teeth-clattering ride.

When I screamed again, I felt Warlock come inside me a second time. He held himself deep, letting his cock pump his cum into my pussy in great jerks. As my body settled, riding the wave back down to earth, Warlock settled himself over me, continuing to kiss me. Gently. His words were now filled with tender praise as he kissed my cheek and neck before ending back at my lips, and he kissed me like I mattered.

"That's my beautiful girl," he murmured. "So responsive. Exactly what I've always wanted in a lover."

He lifted his head, rubbing his nose against mine. I blinked up at him, feeling more vulnerable than I ever had.

"But, what about in everything else?"

He smiled. "You're perfect for me, Hope. The mere fact you haven't asked one of my men here to kill me is proof enough you're perfect for me. This is an added bonus."

"I can't share you, Warlock. If you want another woman, you tell me now."

"I'm not sure which woman here put these thoughts in your head, but I will never stray from you, Hope. I'll never want another woman. Only you. But --" He grinned widely. "-- I'm gonna want you a lot. Every day. Multiple times a day."

The giggle burst out of me. I couldn't help it! Then I remembered. "You came inside me twice. What if I'm pregnant?"

He shrugged. "Since we're already married, I don't see the issue. If you're pregnant, we'll raise the child together."

"OK, then." It settled my mind, but it wasn't everything I wanted. Only time could give me that. But I'd take this. "Together."

"Yeah, baby. Together."

Chapter Eight

Warlock
Christmas Eve

"I am *not* doing this." I really wasn't. Nope. I was not turning in my man card and wearing a fucking Santa suit.

"Oh, come on. It'll be fun." Then Hope went and gave me that fucking brilliant, beautiful smile, and I found myself stripping. Getting ready to put on that fucking Santa suit. Then a wicked thought occurred to me.

"Persuade me." She gave me a confused smile as she undressed for her own Elf costume. I stepped out of my boxer briefs and gripped the base of my cock, giving it a lazy stroke.

Her eyes widened, then she slid her panties down her shapely thighs, stepping out of them on her way to me. When she reached me, instead of wrapping her arms around my neck like I'd expected, she sank to her knees and reached for my cock.

"Ah, hell…" I knew I was in trouble. I held my breath while she brought her mouth to me, taking a tentative lick of the head of my dick. The instant there was contact, my hand shot to her head, my fingers tunneling through her hair. "Fuck!"

That seemed to be her encouragement. Hope sucked me into her mouth. At first, she was tentative, as if she were unsure exactly how to go about it. As she experimented with how to move, she got bolder, until she was sucking as much of my length as she could comfortably take.

"Christ, that feels good!"

"Mmm…" She hummed around my cock, wrapping a delicious vibration around me. The longer she continued, the bolder she became, grabbing my buttocks and kneading as she sucked.

"That's it, Hope. Fuck! So fuckin' good! Suck me down."

She obeyed, taking me as deep as she could. She gagged, but didn't stop. In fact, it seemed to give her courage. She continued, taking me even deeper. She couldn't keep it up for long, but it was long enough for me to realize I'd created a monster. This girl was eager to please me. I wasn't sure I was going to survive this.

"Get up, girl," I growled and pulled her to her feet by her hair. When she met my gaze, there was an almost maniacal gleam in her eyes. "Need to fuck you."

"Yes," she breathed. "Yes, do that."

I turned her around, wrapping one arm around her chest, the other around her waist. My cock found her entrance, and I plunged home. We both groaned. I spread my feet to bring me closer to her level, then I began to fuck her.

The new position seemed to thrill Hope as she panted, gripping my arms and hanging on and letting me have her. Her cries and pants grew louder in our room. I found the side of her neck and fastened my mouth there, which made her gasp and shudder in my arms.

"Fuck, girl! You're a biker's wet dream come true."

"Are you gonna come in me, Max?"

"You bet your sweet ass I'm gonna come in you. Gonna fill you so full…"

"Please! Oh, God! Please, Max! Please!"

Her pleas were the sweetest music. Instantly, my cock swelled, the need to come paramount. I shifted my hold to find her clit and worked it. I was going to come. But, by God, she was going to come first.

The second she clamped down on me and screamed out her orgasm, I unloaded, pumping her full of hot, sticky cum. I held myself as deep as I could, wanting to get it as far inside her as possible. It was a primitive marking. A claim. One I intended to repeat every day for the rest of my life.

When we were both spent, I carried her to the bathroom. I'm not sure how I managed. My legs felt like Jell-O. I sat her on the vanity, then braced my hands beside her hips, lowering my forehead to her shoulder to catch my breath.

"Wow," she said with a chuckle.

"Indeed. Want to stay up here and have our own private Christmas party?"

She pushed me away, giving me a stern look. "That was your persuasion! You have to go with me as Santa now! It's a done deal!" She looked so alarmed, I let out a bark of laughter.

"Mercy on an old man. I'm not gonna be any good at this."

"You'll be wonderful. Besides, Jerrica will be heartbroken if I don't go. And I'm not going without you." She crossed her arms over her chest and gave me an adorable pout.

I gave her a scowl, trying not to laugh and ruin the effect. "Fine. But don't think I don't know you're trying to manage me with sex."

She gave me a bright smile. "As long as we're clear on that." Then she hopped off the counter, wrapping her arms around my neck and giving me a quick kiss before snagging a washcloth. She washed herself and bounded back into the bedroom. I'd never seen anyone so eager for a Christmas party as my girl was.

I grinned. Something had come for me today. Something I was eager to give Hope. And, once again, I had my mother to thank for the timely gift. Damned woman knew me all too well. The years we'd spent apart seemed like a waste now. Both of us too damned stubborn to compromise when we had time. I was glad she had Hope the last few years of her life. She was more than a substitute for me. Hope brought sunshine wherever she went. My mother needed her light as much as I did.

The party was long and degrading. I was pretty sure more than one kid peed on me. I have no idea if it was from excitement or fear, though I tried to smile to take the sting out of my hard features. One boy bullied his way through the line to the front. He was about eight or nine and knew better. I knew so because more than one adult had scolded him. The kid would catch their backs turned and shove the child in front of him out of line until he'd made his way to the front.

He approached me with a cocky smirk. Like he thought getting whatever he wanted was a foregone conclusion. The fact was, in most cases, the kids got exactly what they asked for. Not sure how that worked other than El Diablo was a sneaky bastard. This kid was more than I could take when the only place I wanted to be was upstairs in my room with my cock buried balls-deep in my woman. And I had a present for her that I desperately wanted to give her.

I gave the kid a hard stare. The look I usually reserved for prospects who'd royally fucked up. The boy took one look at me. Did a double take. The color drained from his face, and he promptly puked on my boots. That sent the rest of the line scurrying off. Guess it was time for a break.

"What'd you say to that kid?" Hope's eyes were

big and round.

"Didn't say nothing. But I'm bettin' he doesn't bully his way to the front of the line anymore."

"You realize that's probably gonna get you a lump of coal in your stocking instead of presents. Right?" I nearly laughed out loud at the look of genuine distress on my girl's face.

"Should have known you'd be at the center of any scandal at this party." Wrath approached us with Celeste and their daughters, Holly and Tabitha.

"Not exactly how most of the parties go, but whatever you said, the little shit deserved it." Holly wasn't one to mince words. At eighteen, she already had several men looking her way. Not that her daddy was having any of it. Last word I heard -- as Wrath beat the shit outta some dumbass trying to come on to Holly -- was that Holly wasn't dating until she was at least forty. Unless Wrath was still alive. Then it was fifty.

"Sometimes, all it takes is the right expression." El Diablo sauntered toward us, a grin plastered all over his fucking face. He was dressed immaculately in a tuxedo, Jezebel on his arm in a shimmering emerald-green gown. The thin straps over her shoulders had tiny gems sewn into them. They were probably rhinestones, but I wouldn't bet on it. More likely, they were diamonds and emeralds. Because El Diablo was nothing if not demanding when it came to his woman having the very best.

"Twenty years of wrangling prospects, and I learned the right expression." My comment was a grim reminder to me that was no longer my life.

"Indeed. Which is why I chose you to be Black Reign's enforcer. Life is better all around if the fear of the Devil is put into those around you. You'll be an extension of my wrath." He glanced at Wrath who raised an eyebrow. "No pun intended, of course."

"Uh-huh." Wrath snorted.

"Never said I was takin' that job." The last thing I wanted was for El Diablo to bully me into doing something I didn't want to do.

"So, you're not comfortable with the position?" El Diablo glanced at Wrath, as if the two had been discussing this very thing.

I thought about it a moment. "Not uncomfortable. I don't know if I'm the right fit for the job."

"Rubbish. I saw the look on your face. While I don't condone terrifying young children, as Holly said, the little shit deserved it. That's the look I want my enforcer to have. Saves trouble that way."

"Besides," Jezebel added. "You didn't say anything to him, and you didn't touch him. No harm, no foul." Then she grinned. "*And*, the little shit deserved it. I'll go make sure the kid gets more in his stocking than coal."

"I need to clean up." I stood and snagged Hope's hand. "Come help me change."

"You have fifteen minutes, then I'm sending Wrath after you," El Diablo called out to me as I hurried out of the common room with Hope.

"What are you doing? You don't need my help!" She looked over her shoulder and gestured toward the party. "I'm Santa's Elf! I have to keep the kids entertained while Santa's gone!"

"Relax, sweetheart. It'll only take fifteen minutes. Besides, you've been at it all day. I'm bettin' you need to freshen up."

She turned back to me, narrowing her eyes as we got to the door of our room. "Does freshening up have anything to do with me removing my costume?"

I gave her a lopsided grin. "Only your panties. Been dyin' to see up your skirt all fuckin' day."

I closed the door and hurried to the bathroom to get rid of my boots and pants. Fucking things were ridiculous anyway. When I came back to the bedroom, I reached for her, pulling her skirt up and sliding her panties down her hips. "Max!"

"Shh. Need you, Hope."

I knelt before her -- like she had me. "Pull up that sexy little skirt and let me see my pussy."

As I'd known would happen, her breath hitched, and she opened her lips in an "O" of surprise. She had on a velvet skirt in bright green with some kind of soft, white, fluffy trim that came to above her knees. Likewise, her top matched, with big black buttons trimmed in gold down the front. The bodice showed a modest amount of cleavage, and she'd worn a black choker with a gold snowflake. She had green-and-white-striped stockings that came to below the skirt. Black ankle boots with gold buckles adorned her feet. She was the sexiest Elf I'd ever seen in my life.

She did as I asked, pulling the skirt up to her waist and holding it there. I gripped her thighs and swiped my tongue through her folds. "Fuck! You taste so fuckin' good!"

Her whimper was musical. One hand left her skirt to yank off the damned Santa hat and tunnel through my hair. Since I'd introduced her to sex, Hope had become more assertive about asking for what she wanted. It wasn't always with words, but when she gripped my head to guide my mouth and tongue where she wanted, I understood.

"So good," she gasped. "Don't stop, Max!"

"Mmm…" I flicked her clit over and over,

looking up into her beautiful face as she accepted the pleasure I wanted to give her. When her breathing hitched and I could tell she was about to come, I stood and turned her around so her back was to my front.

"Max!"

"Shh. I'll always take care of you, baby. I'm not gonna leave you hanging."

I guided my cock inside her, pushing through her folds in a slick glide. Wrapping my arms around her, I fucked her hard and fast. My hand wrapped around her delicate throat as I continued to move. As I knew she would, Hope tilted her head back to give me better access.

"Use your fingers to play with your clit. You're gonna come and take me with you."

"Yes! Yes! Fill me up with it!"

Fuck. Me.

It was the first time she'd said anything like that. I knew she was mimicking me, what she thought I'd say. It was hot as fuck.

It didn't take long for her to cry out with her orgasm. She squeezed my dick so fucking good, there was no way I could have held back if I'd wanted to. I didn't want to.

"That's it, baby. That's it! You ready for my cum?"

"Yes! Do it! Do it now!" She screamed as I came inside her. Her hand shot back, and she gripped my ass, digging her fingers into the flesh she found. Her body quivered in my arms. I rested my chin on her shoulder as I continued to come in hot, pulsing spurts.

When it was over, when I finally came back to myself, Hope had a beautiful, contented smile on her face. It was a look I wanted to see every second of every day.

"I think I need to tie you to my bed and keep you there, making love to you."

"I'm not opposed. But it needs to wait until after the party's over." She sighed and turned in my arms.

I leaned down to kiss her tenderly. "Go clean up. Then I've got a present for you."

Her eyes lit up. "A present?" Then she frowned. "But I didn't get you anything."

"Yes, you did." I winked at her. "Now. Go. We've only got a couple minutes before Wrath comes looking for us."

She kissed me once more before hurrying to the bathroom. I walked to my dresser and opened it. Inside, I pulled out a padded envelope. It was addressed to me, but I purposefully left it that way so she could see what it was and where it came from. While I waited, I slung on some jeans and my motorcycle boots. I kept the damned Santa jacket and snagged the hat, but El Diablo was going to have to live with it.

When she came out of the bathroom, she hurried to her dresser and pulled out another pair of panties, stepping into them and sliding them up her hips. I wanted her again. Wanted those shapely thighs gripping my hips as I pounded into her again...

"You ready to go back?" She smiled up at me with more innocence than a woman who'd been railed from behind should be able to pull off. That was my Hope.

"In a minute. First, you need to open your present." I handed her the envelope.

"What's this?"

"Open it."

"But it's addressed to you."

"Yeah, baby. I already opened it." I nodded at

the envelope. "Go ahead. Open it."

She did, taking out the sheet of folded paper and the small box inside. She laid the envelope on the dresser along with the box and opened the letter written in my mother's neat hand.

* * *

My Dearest Maximilian,

> My one great regret in life is that I was too stubborn all these years to see you were right. You were always so attentive to everything going on around you. You saw and heard my frustrations and put in your own plan of action. I couldn't see anything other than you were taking the law into your own hands. That you were doing something I was fundamentally against. I was wrong. If I would have opened my mind and seen your vision... Oh, what a team we would have made.
>
> Anyway. Enough of the musings of an old woman. As I'm sure you know by now, in my will I gave you to my sweet Hope. The girl is aptly named. She gave me hope in my despair and in return, I've done my best to see to it she's taken care of. She's the daughter I never had. While she didn't make up for my wrongs to you, she gave me a second chance to make you happy. She needs a home, Maximilian. A family. So do you. If you give this girl a chance, she will be the best wife you could ever find. She'll give you her whole heart and never question if she should. As long as you're with her, she will be your home.
>
> I purposefully made sure this letter wasn't delivered until Christmas Eve. I wanted

to give you time to get to know her. As I gave you to her as my dying wish, I'm giving her to you for Christmas. I'm sure things started out more than a bit rocky. You never did like it when I meddled in your life. This time, however, I promise you it was necessary. For you both.

Well. You're married to her now. I know you could have gotten it dissolved, but those things take time. Especially when you're out of state. I'm hoping you found it inside you to treat my girl gently. If you did, then everything has worked out. Your wife will need proper engagement and wedding rings. I've enclosed mine. With some slight alterations. (If you knew the lengths I went to in order to get the money for that project, you'd laugh at my hypocrisy. More than a few laws were broken. Blackmail was involved as well.) Put them on her finger and she will wear them with pride, cherishing them always. That's the kind of woman Hope is. You're the kind of man who will protect and cherish her.

I love you both.

Proud mother to a wonderful son and daughter-in-law,

Verna Wagner

* * *

When Hope finished the letter, there were tears streaming down her face. She looked up at me, grief and pain there, but she met my gaze questioningly. Did she still not get it? Was she still insecure with me? I could understand if she was. That would take time, given the way we'd started out.

I smiled gently at her, picking up the jewelry box where she'd set it on the dresser and opening it, taking the rings out. "Give me your hand, sweetheart."

She did, trembling slightly as I slipped first the wedding ring on her finger, then the engagement ring. My mother had had it altered slightly, leaving no mistake she meant for Hope to have it. The diamond was a princess cut. I recognized it as the one my mother always wore. At least she had before I left.

"There's no doubt my mother intended these for you, Hope."

"They're lovely." She sniffed, her voice wavering. Looking up at me, she asked, "Is this what you want? I mean, really? I don't want to trap you, and I feel like Mrs. Wagner did that on my behalf."

"Honey, if she did, she knew what she was doing. I can't go back to not having you in my life. I love you, Hope. I'm glad my mother forced the issue. I wouldn't have it any other way."

With a glad cry, Hope threw herself into my arms, hugging me fiercely. "I love you too, Max! I love you so much!"

Holding her felt too good to let go. I could happily do it all night. Unfortunately, there was a loud knocking at the door. "Time's up, Warlock! Get your Santa-clad ass back to the fuckin' party!"

"Fuuuuck…"

Hope giggled before pulling back, giving me a lingering kiss. "Come on! The kids need Santa and his merry Elf!"

I laughed and followed my woman out the door and back to the party. Kids were every-fucking-where. The things seemed to be multiplying like fucking rabbits! I glanced at Hope where she was already in the middle of a group of them, herding them back to the line for Santa. With a weary sigh, I sat in the chair on the dais the women had decorated in a tacky, gaudy homage to commercialized Christmas.

One at a time, the kids came up to me. Some of them whispered their wishes to me, others were loud and excited. Jezebel took their picture, then I sent them on the way to the huge-ass Christmas tree where Holly and Bella, Rycks and Lyric's daughter, saw to it they all got their presents.

Then Hope led her friend, Jerrica, to me. The child crawled up in my lap shyly and gave me a hug. "I don't need anything for Christmas. I already got everything I wanted."

"You did? Well tell me what you got."

She blinked at me, giving me a puzzled look. "Don't you know? I mean, you gave them to me."

"Uh, sure. But, you know, I need to make sure my elves got it all right."

The child grinned. The explanation on the fly must have worked, which relieved me more than I was comfortable admitting.

"My sister, Iris, got her emancipation papers." She said the word "emancipation" slowly, like she had difficulty with the word. "Once she actually turns eighteen, if she has a steady job and a place to live, the judge said she could adopt me and take me away from the group home." Her smile was bright, and I could see this truly was a glorious thing to this little girl.

"Well, then. Santa will have to make sure Iris has everything she needs to be ready when she turns eighteen."

"Iris can do fine on her own." A young woman stood there, scowling at me. My guess? This was Iris. She was dressed in worn jeans and a T-shirt that looked like it had seen better days. But she was clean.

Except for the smudge of flour on her cheek and nose. "I made you a Christmas cupcake, Jerrica." The second she addressed her younger sister, her expression changed. She smiled eagerly at the girl. "I made you a Christmas cupcake at work today. You want it now?"

"Yeaaaah! We can eat it together." She promptly turned to look up at me. "You want to share too, Santa?"

I padded my belly where the padding made it pooch out. Jolly old Elf and all. "While I appreciate the offer, I need to save room for all the cookies tonight. That one bite of cupcake might push me over the edge, and Rudolph would have a difficult time getting me home." I tried to chuckle with a "Ho, ho, ho," but it came out flat.

Jerrica still grinned, while Iris wrinkled her nose.

"You're a crappy Santa," the older teen muttered. Then led Jerrica away.

"Merry fuckin' Christmas to you," I grumbled. Hope burst out laughing.

"Iris is a handful, but she loves Jerrica more than anything. I'm so happy she got what she needed to be able to start the adoption process with Jerrica. Jezebel says they've both had a rough time since even before their mom died."

"Well, if it makes Jerrica happy, I guess I'll give her a pass. No lump of coal in her stocking."

"You're starting to take this Santa business seriously, then?"

"What? No," I scoffed. "I love the power." I raised an eyebrow. "Am I not merciful?" I reached for Hope and pulled her into my lap. "So, tell me, little girl. What do you want for Christmas?"

She smiled up at me, laying her left hand against my cheek where I knew her rings sparkled under the lights. "I have everything I ever wanted right here."

"You're the best Christmas present I've ever received, Hope. I'll never take you for granted."

"I love you, Max. I love you so much!"

"I love you too, baby. You've brought hope back to my life. My mother was right. You're my Hope in more ways than one."

She gave me that beautiful, dazzling smile. "Then we'll keep each other."

"Forever. For always and ever." I kissed her gently, before pressing my forehead to hers. "Merry Christmas, baby."

"Merry Christmas." Then she hugged me tightly, and I knew it would definitely be a very merry Christmas.

Marteeka Karland

International bestselling author Marteeka Karland leads a double life as an erotic romance writer by evening and a semi-domesticated housewife by day. Known for her down and dirty MC romances, Marteeka takes pleasure in spinning tales of tenacious, protective heroes and spirited, vulnerable heroines. She staunchly advocates that every character deserves a blissful ending, even, sometimes, the villains in her narratives. Her writings are speckled with intense, raw elements resulting in page-turning delight entwined with seductive escapades leading up to gratifying conclusions that elicit a sigh from her readers.

Away from the pen, Marteeka finds joy in baking and supporting her husband with their gardening activities. The late summer season is set aside for preserving the delightful harvest that springs from their combined efforts (which is mostly his efforts, but you can count it). To stay updated with Marteeka's latest adventures and forthcoming books, make sure to visit her website. Don't forget to register for her newsletter which will pepper you with a potpourri of Teeka's beloved recipes, book suggestions, autograph events, and a plethora of interesting tidbits.

Bones MC Multiverse: changelingpress.com/bones-mc-u-13

Marteeka at Changeling: changelingpress.com/marteeka-karland-a-39

Changeling Press E-Books

More Sci-Fi, Fantasy, Paranormal, and BDSM adventures available in e-book format for immediate download at ChangelingPress.com -- Werewolves, Vampires, Dragons, Shapeshifters and more -- Erotic Tales from the edge of your imagination.

What are E-Books?

E-books, or electronic books, are books designed to be read in digital format -- on your desktop or laptop computer, notebook, tablet, Smart Phone, or any electronic e-book reader.

Where can I get Changeling Press E-Books?

Changeling Press e-books are available at ChangelingPress.com, Amazon, Apple Books, Barnes & Noble, and Kobo/Walmart.

ChangelingPress.com

Printed in Great Britain
by Amazon